Mena Dhu

Published under licence by Brown Dog Books and
The Self-Publishing Partnership, 7 Green Park Station, Bath BA1 1JB

www.selfpublishingpartnership.co.uk

ISBN printed book: 978-1-83952-145-4
ISBN e-book: 978-1-83952-146-1

Cover design by Andrew Prescott
Internal design by Andrew Easton

Printed and bound by CPI Group (UK) Ltd, Croydon CR0 4YY

This book is printed on FSC certified paper

Mena Dhu

A Cornish Comedy

Tony Cottrell

BROWN
DOG
BOOKS

Chapter One

On the headland to the west of Porthwallow Bay, on the south coast of Cornwall, completely hidden by a forest of trees, sits, reputedly, the ancient house, Mena Dhu. It means 'Black Hill' in Cornish because that is how the headland looks from the sea with the setting sun behind it. Very few ordinary people have actually seen it, as the clever planting of the trees has, over the generations, rendered it virtually invisible from all sides, even the sea. Possibly the most determined of geeks with these new drone things might be able to video its roofs but then, one roof is pretty much like another. Old twisted oaks like the wildest Disney fantasies make up most of the barrier, with birch filling the skyline and an impenetrable undergrowth below. There are pathways through but they are only known to the retainers who care for them in a seemingly haphazard way. Hopeful rubber-neckers who hire boats and boatmen may just catch a glimpse of rooftops and chimney pots on a winter's day but for most people, they have to take the locals' word for its existence, rather like that of there having once been decent weather in August.

Legend has it that Daphne du Maurier lived there for a while and that it must have acted as inspiration for 'Manderley,' but if Miss du Maurier had actually lived in all the houses she is supposed to have done, she would never have written anything, except lists for the removal men. Visitors are not encouraged, partly due to the current owner, young Lord Cosmo de Coverlet's one-time predilection for disporting himself in various stages of exotic dress around the grounds, sometimes accompanied by well-built, even scantier-clad young ladies, when he could afford them, often around quarter days when the rents came in. 'Young', though, is all relative, as he is nearly fifty and disporting is a young man's pass time.

"It's no good," he said one morning to Hives, the butler, who was serving him breakfast from the array of chaffing dishes on top of the ancient oak sideboard. This magnificent piece of furniture is reputed to have been 'rescued' from a fine East Indiaman which had come to grief on the rocks below the house on the return journey from the Orient in the middle of the 18th century.

Fortunately, the captain had managed to beach this treasure chest of a ship, laden as she was with spices and silks as well as gold, silver bullion and jewels, on the spit of sand just in the break in the rocks that constituted Marth Strand, immediately below Mena Dhu, thereby saving her from too much damage. All the crew and passengers had clambered ashore and up to the Big House, an achievement that earned the captain even more esteem; however, the fact that it also gave the people from the Big House comparatively easy access to the ship, putting them hours ahead of other locals from nearby Porthwallow in the stripping of the contents was never mentioned. But, once the storm had passed and while waiting the next high tide to float her off, carpenters from the house managed to remove this sideboard and other furnishings from the Captain's cabin. These had graced the Big Dining Room at Mena Dhu ever since.

It was only after the third such wreck, under the same master and most of the same crew, that it became known that he had been brought up as a boy in nearby Fowey and used to sail into the cove regularly to set his lobster pots. He was dismissed from the East India Company immediately and no other merchant would consider employing him but, by then, he was wealthy enough to buy one of the quayside inns in Porthwallow and enjoy a very happy retirement, a regular guest for dinner with whichever of the de Coverlets lived in the Big House at the time and had benefited from the 'disasters'.

The word 'wreck' is never used in Mena Dhu, nor anywhere else along the Cornish coast. No evidence has ever been found of anyone setting false lights to lure ships on to the rocks and, for the most part, the locals helped rescue the mariners before stripping the wreck of whatever was portable. Some popular novels and subsequent television dramatisations may have suggested the contrary but it just wasn't true. Or at least, not so recorded by participants.

"No," repeated Lord Cosmo, dressed in his usual breakfast attire of Arabic *thawb*, Aladdin-style slippers and his favourite red-velvet smoking cap, "Things are going to have to change!"

"Not your breakfast, surely, Lord Cosmo?"

"What? No, no. Breakfast as usual, please, Hives."

He spread his wide linen napkin across his not-so-slight belly, tucked it into the neck of the *thawb* and contemplated with relish the meal before him.

He had fallen in love with Morocco after seeing 'Casablanca' and this explained his taste for Arabic clothing. However, this whole *'affaire'* was shattered when he had discovered that the entire film had be made on the back lots of Hollywood, with the exception of the air field scenes, which were shot nearby at Van Nuys Airport, Los Angeles.

His small bowl of prunes, which he did not particularly enjoy, were a homage to an especially well-endowed Nanny who had once looked after him: "Keep your botty happy," she would say, "and the rest will follow." The memory of that starched blouse buttoned up to the neck and the movement beneath it could still arouse excitement in him, even though it would have been more than forty years ago. The waffles and blueberries were a habit picked up while in the States, from eating in those endless, identical motels as he drove Route 66, on one of the several occasions that he was rusticated from Oxford. The scrambled egg and crispy bacon were simple, personal pleasures. The fact that all the other chaffing dishes were brimming with fried eggs, local sausages *and* chipolatas, black pudding, Hogs pudding- a Duchy delicacy, favourite of Tonkin, the gardener- back bacon *and* crispy streaky bacon, baked beans, fried potatoes, hash browns- another novelty brought back with the waffle- and mushrooms was not a problem, for once Cosmo had had his granary toast and a scrape of Marmite to go with the scrambled eggs, all was cleared away to the kitchen where the staff fulfilled an invaluable task of ensuring that there was no waste. With Mr Hives at the head and Cook at the foot of the kitchen table, there was a half-hour of relative peace, disturbed only by champing, the rattle of Tonkin's dentures and Monica, the little maid's endless round from table to range to fill the various tea and coffee pots, each suited to its owner's predilection. The guarantee of clearance had been augmented recently by the admittance of two Polish labourers who did much of the heavy work in the gardens and woodland.

What had been troubling the future master of the house was his place in history, particularly the history of his family.

"What's that thing in the Bible about putting off childish things?"

Hives inhaled pleasurably and recited: "'When I was a child, I spake as a child, I understood as a child, I thought as a child; but when I became a man, I put away childish things. For now we see through a glass, darkly, but then face to face'. Some of King James' finest, if I may say so, sir."

Cosmo looked up from his plate.

"Oh, you don't think he actually wrote the stuff himself, do you, Hives?"

"I did like to think so, sir, seated in the Bloody Tower but I imagine in fact he had a team of scholars and scribes."

Cosmo looked out of the window to the sea below.

"I used to think it meant he had a toy cupboard and had

had to put away childish things, but now I realise it wasn't being quite so... ah... "He sought for the word.

"Literal, milord?"

"Thank you, Hives. Literal."

Hives was a little worried.

"Were there any particular childish things you were anxious to put away? Surely not the space hoppers, sir? When it's wet, they are sometimes the only exercise we can get, up and down the portrait gallery."

"No, Hives, I'm possibly not choosing my words very well..." He was ready to apologise to anyone if he felt he had wronged them.

"But they are splendid words, if I may say so."

"Thank you, but what with the Pater at death's door..." Hives made a preventive gesture, not exactly the sign of the cross, for he had been brought up a Baptist, but certainly more than for just indigestion.

"I do hope not, sir..."

"Good of you to say so, "said Cosmo as he wiped some maple syrup from his chin, " but he has got to the stage like that poor soul in 'Catch Twenty Two'- simply swapping the what-goes-in bottle with the what-comes-out bottle every few hours. Hardly need the two nurses we employ- a plumber could do the job."

"Probably be more expensive, sir."

"Hadn't thought of that, but, no- I don't begrudge the old bugger those gals, but... well, how long do you think your sperm lasts?"

Hives was rarely lost for an answer to the most remarkable of his master's questions but this one threw him temporarily.

"My... ah. My sperm? Well, I haven't had much opportunity..." whereupon Sir Cosmo stopped him.

"No, no, not yours personally. I was meaning in general, like the German 'Man'. One's sperm."

Hives was rather relieved with this explanation.

"Well, very variable, I should imagine. In your father's case, I presume such ah- 'issue' to be highly unlikely. But if the... author... is fit and well, well, one hears stories of fatherhood being granted at a great age. Even ignoring the Bible and all of those ridiculous Patriarch's ages, a hundred has been recorded, I believe. Is there any special reason that you need to know, Sir?"

"No, no it's just that... well, I feel that it's about time I knocked out my heir and a spare myself, don't you know?"

Hives was shocked.

"Fatherhood?!"

"And that," said Monica, the sparrow-chested maid, to the assembled ladies of the staff around the kitchen table, "was when Mr Hives sent me out."

"Good Lord!- and I don't mean his Lordship!" said Mrs Walker, the housekeeper; she was always a blaze of colour, usually reds and yellows, echoing her chubby, Worcester Pearmain of a face.

"Can't stand black," she would say, "Gives a girl that washed-out, more-dead-'n-alive look, know what I mean?"

Even on formal occasions, her uniform was a maroon dress, complete with a Cornish tartan sash. She was a cuddly soul who sat at Mr Hives' right-hand during staff meals.

They had an agreement.

They both had rooms of their own, Mrs Walker's being in the staff wing along with Cook, Nanny, the maids such as Monica and the nurses but if, as seemed most unlikely, she was needed in the night, more often than not she could be found with Mr Hives, in what had been old Lord Cosmo's dressing room but which had been converted into a comfy put-you-up and gave access to the rooms of both old and young Lord Cosmos on either side in case of need.

The doors had been especially sound-proofed and were rarely opened.

Tonkin had his own cottage somewhere in the woods while young Tom Salt, who doubled as gardener's boy and 'Boots', had his bed in the stables, as it was felt unfair on him to be expected to withstand the temptation from so much female flesh in the staff wing of Big House and that the horses would offer a different sort of company. No-one was too sure of the whereabouts of the Poles' sleeping quarters.

Back in the dining room, Sir Cosmo and Hives were in deep and serious conversation. It would have been evident to the observer that it was serious because Hives had actually sat down, an outward sign that he had changed roles from faithful butler to surrogate father figure.

Even in their younger years, old Lord Cosmo had always found it difficult to talk to his son. He had had no trouble in addressing hundreds at the Royal Society when lecturing in Truro Museum on his hobby, the serpentine stone of the Lizard Peninsula, something about which he knew a great deal, but when it came to fatherhood, something about which he knew very little, he preferred to say nothing, rather than make mistakes. He left his son to do that on his own. And Hives was usually there to pick up the pieces.

"Do you have anyone in mind, milord?"

"Good lord, no! You remember that Jane Austen thing? About a single man in possession of a good fortune must want a wife? Load of old tosh. Last thing I wanted was some Rodean reject getting in me way. But that was then, since when, I must admit, I have been thinking."

"Well, that's admirable, milord. Can one ask about what?"

Cosmo was very open about the answer.

"Oh, the usual thing, Hives. My usual thing. Breasts." Hives nodded sagely.

"When it comes to a wife, what would their primary function be? Indeed, what *should* their primary function be?"

Very little fazed Hives. He thought and then replied: "Well, if one is to go by the book, feeding the son and heir, but in moments such as these, I don't think one should approach the matter like a military manoeuvre- Remember? Purpose, objectives and tasks? Training concept, tactical engagement simulation exercise-"

"Ah, the old TASEX, I remember it well- during my brief stay at Sandhurst," muttered Cosmo but failing to interrupt Hives' thought pattern.

"Finishing with a Live Firing exercise. As I say, sir- these are not, in my humble opinion, the way to go about things. May do for the Taliban in Helmand province but there are other ways in the Home Counties, especially when it comes to young women."

Cosmo's eyes lit up but not with pleasure.

"A terrible thought has just struck me, Hives."

"My lord?"

"Will I have to get rid of my magazines?"

This, indeed, was something of a dichotomy. While a wife-to-be would probably be somewhat nonplussed were she to open the glass doors fronting Cosmo's special set of shelves in the library to discover, neatly bound, every copy of Playboy since its first edition, back in December 1953 with Marilyn Monroe as centrefold, she would need to be made aware of their value. That copy alone (and Cosmo had, over the years, bought several) was worth more than $5000, and the whole collection, in its own way, was indicative of something about the American male, although no-one was exactly sure what.

"Surely an American university library would buy the lot?" suggested Cosmo. "After all, they offer degrees in surfing and underwater basket-making. Maybe those students could use some time in the library..." This was not sarcasm so much as an honest observation.

"I am sure that we could find some mid-western establishment that has not succumbed totally to political correctness and could see them as a sociological manifestation, rather than mild pornography. We could advertise in the Times Education Supplement."

"Higher Ed."

"Indeed, milord."

"Can one do the same thing for wives, these days? Something in the back pages of 'the Lady'?"

"I really don't know, sir" replied Hives. " But I will look into it."

Chapter Two

⁓

Porthwallow is just one of several small fishing villages that have clung to the south east coast of Cornwall like the limpets that their inhabitants were reduced to eating when times were hard.

Way back, the ancestors probably scraped a living on the sea's edge even before they developed the art of boat building. Suitable logs would be swept down the rivers or be dragged out of the woodland by the more entrepreneurial of the Iron Age inhabitants. They developed a sort of sea-going coracle and as their metal implements developed, so did the quality of their sea-going craft and the variety of what they could catch from them. As their building skills improved, so did the safety of their havens. While some villagers out west may still to this day draw their boats out of the tide's reach daily, others wanted things a little safer and a little easier, and so quays and harbour walls, even moles like Looe's Banjo Pier were built and the boats kept from the fury of the sea. Porthwallow made do with a harbour wall.

And all this while, they went after the pilchards.

This harvest could be almost Biblical. True, tin had brought traders from as far away as the Holy Land and some include Jesus Christ, with his uncle, Joseph of Arimathea, as being among the young metal brokers. Footprints solidified in the clay near to Penzance are claimed by particularly ardent proselytes to be actual impressions of those feet that were so cruelly dealt with later on, but these adherents are fairly few. There were also references to Pontius Pilate having come this way by way of mortification but when one sees the way his legend is treated in some of the medieval Miracle plays, little credence should be given here too.

Later, the discovery of china clay above St. Austell was another unique source of riches for the Cornish mine owners, including the de Coverlets; but the pilchard, one of the humble herring family so beloved of Europeans from Sweden to Portugal, often given the soubriquet of 'sardine' to tart it up a bit, was a vast source of staple food and basic income for the inhabitants of Porthwallow and their neighbours along the South Cornish coast.

And these colossal shoals would exude oil, Omega-3 rich oil; the natives were sadly ignorant of their eicosapentaenoic acid content, as well as the benefit to their cholesterol profile; what they did know was there was a lot of them, easy to catch and tasty to eat. They even created a gastronomic masterpiece, the stargazy pie, into which as the name suggests, the pilchards were put and baked, whole, with their heads poking through the pastry, gazing at the stars.

So many fish all squeezing themselves together meant that they gave off oil without meaning to. The massive oil slicks on the surface of the waves above them revealed their presence below and watchers, known as 'huers', on the cliffs along the coast would call out to the people below and direct the boats.

As soon as the fish were seen, all other activity would cease in the village, save getting as much of these silver riches from the sea to the land. Nets were by far the most popular means but there were stories of shovelling the catch from the sea into the holds by basket or even by spade. Off-loading was the same; the majority of the catch was packed tail to tail in barrels and sent away to Greece, Spain and Portugal, once the locals' own needs were salted away in their cellars. Down the ages, with machinery, the pilchard canning factory was developed and most villages had at least one such plant, usually near to the sea so that the inevitable effluent could go out with the tide.

The so-called March on London, lauded in Hawker's 'Song of the Western Men'-

"And shall Trelawny live,

Or Shall Trelawny die,

Here's twenty thousand Cornishmen

Shall know the reason why."

probably never took place at all because it was pilcharding time and folk had their priorities right.

The weather early summer, 1588, had been, and continued to be, dreadful and the organisers of the East Cornwall and Plymouth and District Bowls league were tearing their hair out for dry days to fit in the postponed league matches.

July 20th was a Saturday (Julian Calendar) and the game between *The Whitchurch Inn,* near Tavistock, Francis Drake's local, and *The Fisherman's Arms,* in Plymouth had been rearranged several times and finally agreed upon that date. Because the pub was built into the walls of the castle, they played their home matches out on Plymouth Hoe.

The bowdlerized version of Drake's remarks about the Spanish Armada, sailing by just off the Eddystone at the time, is well-known.

What is less well-known is the fact that, on the same day, the team from *The de Coverlet Arms* in Porthwallow, a comparatively new establishment, was taking on *The Crown* at Lanlivery, one of the oldest pubs in Cornwall. The then Cosmo de Coverlet had managed to raise a team and, what was more impressive, to get them up to Lanlivery and so no minor interruption, such as the possible invasion of the realm by the Spanish Armada, was going to interrupt their game. By the time they had got back home again, pleasantly drunk, in the early hours of the next morning, a Sunday, they were in no mind to go to sea, summed up in a comment, less well known than that of Drake but equally apposite, from Lord de Coverlet: " Olay, Olay, Olay, Olay! We beat *The Crown*. That's what really matters round here. I can't be arsed to get in a bloody boat and chase those wretched Dagoes. We'd never catch up with them anyway. Oggie, oggie, oggie, oi, oi, oi!!".

The Great Unpleasantness, better known as the Civil War, did impinge somewhat upon Porthwallow when there were battles and skirmishes all round inland. Both Mena Dhu and the village were staunchly Royalist but given that the de Coverlets' claim to the Crown was greater than that of King Charles, they kept this fairly quiet, so as not to attract the attention of the Roundheads. The added incentive of keeping what lay in their Endowment Room secret made them even less enthusiastic. This was made easier after the defeat in August 1644 of the Parliamentarian army at nearby Castle Dor, when the officers abandoned their men and escaped by boat from Fowey to Plymouth, leaving the ordinary men to make their own way home.

None of them did, for two major reasons: the high banked lanes made it impossible for strangers to know where they were going- a problem faced by emmets today, even with Sat Navs- or especially with Sat Navs- and the men, armed mainly with, and completely hampered by, 16ft long pikes, were unable to turn round in the lanes to defend themselves and so were slaughtered by the locals, the ladies with their gutting knives to the fore. Pike heads were to be seen for generations to come as, variously, axes, boathooks and scythes.

Sadly though for the Royalists, King Charles the First suffered from that ailment seen in both the great and the lesser in the land, that of being both big-headed yet narrow-minded at the same time. The disparity between the two was probably filled with self-esteem. He was such a blockhead that it was quite apposite that that was how he died, his head on the executioner's block. However, this act of effrontery on the part of the Parliamentarians had little effect in Cornwall.

Mena Dhu

The major event in and around Porthwallow was the decision of the then Lord de Coverlet to knock down the old manor house, known for centuries as Tristan's Leap, and build what was to become arguably the finest Jacobean great house in the Duchy. Building had been interrupted when there were actual armies meandering about the county in the early Forties, but it was continued once Charles' execution had put an end to such interruptions.

Mena Dhu is built on three sides of a square but really only inhabited now in the main section. Servants live in the West wing and no-one is very sure what to do with the vast reception rooms of the East Wing. Very few of the de Coverlets were particularly enthusiastic dancers and most fulfilled their obligation as host for the Hunt Ball when their turn came around with little joy. For the more practical among them, it gave them a chance to empty their wine cellars of the undrinkable, viewing most of their neighbouring gentry as graceless dolts on whom the better vintages would have been wasted. Similarly, the 'cooking' hardly deserved the name as they slaughtered several cattle and burned them to a lesser or greater degree in the vast fireplace. It was only the pasties and the stargazy pies that generations of cooks bothered to exert themselves over, and few of the guests noticed the difference.

True, the East Wing did house the Long gallery, or Picture gallery, scene of moments of intimate in-house games and some of the reports of indoor cricket, if true, should have reached the ears of the MCC at Lords.

There was a particular scion of the family, before the Great War, who was reputed to have hit the bust of William the Third full-tilt from the other end of the room three times in a row. True, the bowler was a very personable young housemaid who was said to do anything to please the young master but even so, it took a remarkable eye. Sadly, he lost it on the Somme.

The Great War insidiously affected everyone, as everyone knew someone who had marched away, many on that very day in August 1918, when war was declared, and who had never marched home again. The gardeners and grooms in particular at Mena Dhu had enlisted '*en masse*', forming their own little pals' battalion, which meant that the grounds ran wild and the family had to clean their own boots and curry their own horses for years.

During the Second World War, in 1940, the one enemy plane that those on watch did spot from their Observation Post- a converted pig-sty on the cliffs- had obviously been flown by a windy bunch, for no sooner had they crossed the coast and seen the blacked-out glow of Plymouth, some thirty miles away, than they dumped their bombs willy-nilly and as one of the witnesses had said at the time: "Then the Focker fucked off out of 'ere."

The pig-sty held no pigs, because of its converted wartime use but the bomb did manage to kill a sheep and traumatise dozens more and every spring at ploughing time for years to come, farmers would dig up bits of green-painted bomb casing, but fortunately no human was hurt. The Home Guard corporal, Iggy Holmes, used to tell the story for the price of several pints of rough cider.

"We see'd 'ee, see, and us was arguing as to whether this was the right opportune time to use our one bullet- us had several rifles but only the one bullet 'tween us, see? Rations- but by the time us 'ed made up our minds, the bugger was 'ere, there, dropped 'is lot and gone. All us could do was duck. Mind you, what Fritz was thinkin' of, bombin' a pigsty, I can't imagine- less'n it was all part a' 'itler's Grand Plan, tryin' to starve us out, gradual-like. Pigsty by pigsty. I mean, rations was short, but a coupla pigs weren't gonna make all that diff'rence to the War Effort. Not in the long run."

By the time Jago and Hezekiah went fishing, the days of glut were long gone. Somehow, the same always seemed to happen with Cornwall's assets, be it tin, copper, china clay, fish, even holiday-makers, all were over-exploited, by the owners, leaving the people to starve or emigrate; many took the latter course. And still do. But not our pair.

True, Jago had been away but he had come back. Hezekiah had spent a few wild years down West, doing what he could to make ends meet. Some say he learned his building techniques down there but he had come back, with a lovely Camborne girl, Jessie, in tow and soon he had a family to support.

Mena Dhu

Between them, H. and Jago had bought an old 24-foot fishing boat, named it the *Jessie-Nicole* for obvious reasons and they would go out after whatever was still out there and sell it at Looe market.

As holiday makers replaced the indigenous, they took to taking them fishing, or simply for a ride, telling them the history of the area, or, in the case of Jago, making up whatever fantastical version of the truth came into his fertile mind. For the visitors, a trip round the bay became something of a must, often rounded off by the privilege of buying several pints in *The de Coverlet Arms,* for their newly-befriended nautical guides. To be seen, perched on a bar stool alongside of Jago Hocking *was* the height of achievement for many, men and women alike, and they never realised that the performance would be likely to be the same, equally exclusive, for the next lot of emmets to be down next week.

The one occupation that was not driven into the ground by greedy bosses was occasional smuggling. Some said that it had died out in the Nineteenth century but there were regular reports of its resurgence and only last year, Porthwallow had consciously resorted to it in their hour of need.

It was definitely not as much in demand these days as it was backalong, what with Social Security and that, but at the end of the eighteenth century, a couple of ships sailing out of Porthwallow would join the Fowey Gallants , the Looe luggers and the fleet of Polperro gaffers where it was claimed that every household was actively involved. Even the children, taught expressly by Zepheniah Job, knew how to add and subtract and keep the books for their innumerate parents.

In Porthwallow, as in much of Cornwall, it was an opportunity for the whole community, village, church and Mena Dhu, to work together.

Being miles down lanes that were virtually impassable on horseback and even less so by carriage, it was unlikely that the Revenue Officers ever bothered to investigate the villagers by land, but there was always the sea, where the Revenue cutters were a hated sight. The men that manned them were no less detested and Israel Couch, the landlord of *The de Coverlet Arms* at the time, refused to serve those who did ever make it to shore.

Methodism had not really taken its restrictive hold on the Church of England by then and the incumbent, the Reverend Henry Chetwood was a welcome guest, both at the dinner table at Mena Dhu and the public bar of *The de Coverlet Arms*. This was mainly because he was a cheery soul and as *'bon'* a *'viveur'* as you could wish to meet. But he, unknown to anyone today, had been an innocent precursor of today's Reverend Trevor: whereas Trevor had only cemented his position with the locals by lending the empty rear of the nave for their fund-raising activity, so Henry, in return for the traditional barrels of brandy, had allowed access to a fairly empty crypt for temporary storage and distribution of certain goods. The permanent occupants were certainly not likely to bear witness.

Chapter Three

Cosmo's had not been a normal upbringing. Up until the age of five, his education had been in the hands of a succession of Nannies, chosen by his mother for their fierceness and propriety, which laid down a basic fear of the opposite sex in young Cosmo. Sadly, to escape the outbreak of influenza in Britain in the early 1970s, his mother had taken the boy to Venice, where she had died of cholera.

This was an unfortunate hiatus in the life of his Lordship. But he too had a Hives of his own to fall back on; the father of Cosmo's factotum had a relationship with the old lord similar to that enjoyed by his current offspring now.

The only difference- and a big one at that- was that the older Hives had been through the Second World War with the current lord's grandfather. Using his 'special circumstances' with the Crown, his then Lordship had been able to insist that the then Hives serve alongside him in the 9th Lancers during the battle of El Alamein and the long liberation of Italy. One of the many benefits of this experience, along with a consummate knowledge of the better Italian wines, was that Hives senior could swear in almost every Italian dialect that ever there was and to hear this torrent of profanity from the lips of a very correct English gentleman removed whatever obstacle any gondolier, taxi driver, hearse handler or porter might try to put in his way of returning the coffin of her Ladyship to England. Lord de Coverlet had sent the current nanny- she of the welcoming chest- with Hives to look after the boy, which she had done. Whether she had offered similar, possibly more adult care to the butler on the way out, nobody knows.

His mother had been one of those flighty, lissom young 'gals' on the edge of Princess Margaret's set, blue blood mixed with Martinis in the veins and no money in the bank, an *habituee* of Carnaby Street and the Colony Club. His father, now lying doped and dormant in the West Wing, had met her briefly on one of his rare excursions to the capital, where he had lost his way *en route* from the family town house in Grosvenor Square to the House of Lords, one day when he had decided to walk. She was stunning and knew how to stun.

Having soon learned that this inauspicious bumpkin's wealth probably exceeded that of the Duke of Westminster, she decided to make herself sufficiently fascinating that he could not avoid proposing before being taken to her bed. After the wedding, she continued with her London life while he, aware that he had done his duty, returned to Mena Dhu and paid the bills. She came to visit often enough to conceive the current Sir Cosmo and then unfortunately had chosen Venice as a haven from the 'flu.

Cosmo did not really miss his mother, as she had insisted on living in Grosvenor Square while his father, the head of the de Coverlet domain, preferred to oversee everything very quietly from the Big House overlooking Porthwallow Bay.

But he had noticed a change in the ladies employed to bring him up. Younger, cheerier and even to Cosmo's young eyes, more rounded in those places where the previous governesses had been rigidly restrained. They tended not to stay long, any of them, but they all left on amiable terms with their employer who had even been known to tap one or two on their light-brown-clad backsides as they were leaving. Whether any of them were more intimate with him than this, no-one knows and given the size of their leaving presents and subsequent pensions, no-one was telling. The last, Nanny Thomlinson, was different; she was a homely, companionable soul who stayed on, 'just in case' to offer some sort of continuity, once it was known that Cosmo was to go off to school; she was older than the rest, nearer the age of her employer.

With no mother to argue his case against being sent to prep. school, it was a '*fait accompli*'. His father, Lord Cosmo- the family tradition of calling all the first-born and hence future Lords the same as those past, namely 'Cosmo', originated several centuries before by an arrogant but uninspired ancestor, was confusing to most people- had been sent to the Dragon School in Oxford during the War and in so far as it can be said that he had ever obviously enjoyed anything, seemed to have been happy enough to insist that his son be sent there.

The school, on the banks of the Isis at Oxford, was something of an idyll. It was as though the pupils, in their blue corduroy shorts, were permanently auditioning for a never-ending production of 'Lord of the Flies'. Under the then Headmaster, 'Jock' Lynam, it was full of every example of upper-middle class boy that you could think of and some that, thankfully, you could not. And the occasional girl who was looked upon as an honorary boy, the only difference being the length of their hair and the way they pissed.

All of these things were noted by young Cosmo and he loved his time at school, so it came as something of a shock when he was moved on to Eton, where many of these pleasures were denied him. There were various things that he could find in Windsor but somehow, with all the big boys about, hinting at all sorts of forbidden pleasures, Cosmo was uncertain as to which way to go- establishment or rebel.

So he became a rebellious member of the Establishment, something that he could remain without too much activity. Becoming an established member of the rebellion, any rebellion, remained both dangerous and unthinkable.

Which was fortunate, as a serious rebel in his unique position, given who he probably was, could have seriously rocked the national and indeed international boat; but he simply retained the status quo, which, as any serious sailor will tell you, can often take far more delicate skills.

Sex at Mena Dhu was dealt with in the Edwardian manner. What had been good enough for the current Lord de Coverlet's grandfather, father and self was deemed the way to go for young Cosmo, along with his cousin Philip, who had this thing about cars: he was being a De Lorean at the time.

Cousin Philip was, it must be admitted, a little unusual, especially in his obsession with cars, whose essence he would adopt implicitly. But it was the benign way in which he looked at the world and led his life that had drawn him to the attention of some of the panjandrums of the Foreign Office. It was almost as though he was too good for this world and that the world had set out to prove it.

The FO was an ideal environment for what some called 'eccentricity' and others 'insanity'. His procurement of the cocaine in Bolivia to help the funding of the new Village Hall for Porthwallow, elsewhere related, had been only one such triumph.

His earliest heroic failure had been during his time in the Caribbean when helping to organise a royal tour, he had booked a visit for Her Majesty at a local factory, only to discover that it produced and was determined to display, exotic ladies' underwear, not deemed suitable for the royal couple.

It was he who had provided the briefing notes for his namesake, Prince Philip, in China when he had described the capital as 'ghastly' and the backing of the opposition's animal in a camel race in Saudi Arabia very nearly caused him to lose his head.

And a very unprepossessing head it was, too. He was taller than cousin Cosmo, very nearly six foot but while Sir Cosmo was rather old-fashioned, favouring the shoulder-length locks and goatee beard of some of his earlier ancestors, Philip could almost have been described as an 'egg-head' in its smoothness, although 'potato-head' was more suited.

He wore suits, as prescribed by the FO but he did add a touch of individuality with his brothel creepers which he sometimes referred to as his 'wheels' and his invariably unmatching fluorescent socks. He was not married.

In their time, their recent ancestors had all either been taken or been sent to Paris for the express purpose of losing their virginities. No-one knew or thought to ask whether any of them had beaten their Parisian trips, organised by their fathers, to it, either with an obliging member of staff or one of the local peasantry, who doubtlessly would have been more than willing to accommodate at half the price and in their native tongue, but the Paris trip had become an entrenched milestone in the upbringing of a de Coverlet; the current Sir Cosmo's father and uncle, Philip's father- something of a late developer- having been the last, sometime in the early Fifties. But, one day in 1985, His Lordship had called the boys to the Accounts' Room which acted as his study, where they were surprised to see him holding a telephone, a thing he rarely used.

"Just checking. You boys free the weekend after next?"

They could neither of them think of an objection and so he opened an old and battered pocket diary, checked the number and proceeded to dial slowly.

When the call was answered, he spoke in a slow but correct French, in an accent reminiscent of Edward Heath arguing for the EEC.

"'Allo, est-ce que Madame Fifi est la? ... Fifi, c'est ..." And here he lowered his voice. "C'est... Momo a l'appareil'... Oui, c'est ça, ton petit Momo." He cleared his throat again. "Oui, c'est lontemps que je ne t'ai pas vue, moi non plus..." And he continued to arrange for the boys' excursion.

Cosmo came back with a dose of the flu' while Philip had fallen in love with a Citroen Traction Avant, as used by Inspector Maigret.

This traditional interview between father and son being over, the young Cosmo was more than surprised to be summoned to the Accounts Room again not long after his return from Paris.

His father was sufficiently caring to ask after the well-being of Madame Fifi who had obviously made a considerable impression on him all those years ago. Young Cosmo replied that she seemed ... "well-preserved" was the word he chose but went on to explain that they had not seen that much of her as their education had been trusted to some of her younger *protegees*.

"Yes," said the older man. "Yes, I suppose... when you come to think about it, which in all honesty, I don't... much, she would seem... older. But that was not what I have to tell you."

Here he stopped, pushed his spectacles back to the bridge of his nose and appeared to be lost in thought.

"My boy, now that you have... endured that... um... element of every man's upbringing- or at least what should be part of his upbringing, and there is every likelihood that you will, one day, inherit... No, no, no false protestation... everything is obviously in working order... at least that's what Fifi has reported back to me- she is less certain about Philip- but I digress... no, it is time that you should be told... ah... told."

As his father did not seem to invite interruption, Cosmo sat and waited.

"You will probably have noticed these fine old chests." Here he pointed to the dark, ancient chests that were almost invisible in the dimmest, farthest corner of the room.

"They contain possibly the most valuable and certainly the most... ah... explosive material in this country and, again, arguably the world. Now there's nothing to be worried about. Much. I shall come on to the other box in a minute, but the coffer contains what is essentially proof that we, the de Coverlets, have ah- inalienable rights to the crown of England and therefore most likely, of the entire United Kingdom, once the others joined in."

This time, Cosmo's silence was one of stupefaction, rather than obedience.

"Yes, bit of a bomb-shell. Essentially, I am more rightfully monarch of this realm than Auntie Betty and you, the more proper heir than... well, than any of them."

As Cosmo seemed incapable of speech, his father continued.

"I'll take you through it all one day but that's probably

enough for now. Let me just say that, obviously, you do not discuss this with anyone, not even Hives; and that in the other, well, it seems it's the body of King Arthur. THE King Arthur."

It was no surprise that Cosmo, having learned what he had learned, lived in something of a state of confusion.

Oxford was, again, a bit of a curate's egg. Much of it Cosmo loved: the back streets off the High, the Magdalene College deer park and the Botanical Gardens over the road, Jericho, even the Bodleian Library, with the exception of those sections in which he was supposed to be studying.

No-one at Eton had been able to discover any particular academic enthusiasm in Cosmo; in fact, no particular enthusiasm at all. He was more than capable at most subjects and had chosen, as two to be studied for 'A' level, Mandarin Chinese and Global Development. He felt that the Chinese probably held the future of the world in their billions of hands. He had considered Quantitative Research but when he saw its definition: 'the systematic empirical investigation of observable phenomena via statistical, mathematical or computational techniques', and realised that he did not even understand the description, he felt that there was little likelihood of him grasping the matter in any depth.

There was a similar problem when he went up to Christchurch; the de Coverlets had endowed a scholarship more than 500 years ago and so there was no problem in him getting in, nor finding that the favourite set of rooms on Tom Quad were made available.

The question was: what was he going to read?

A passing fluency in Chinese, little more, was all he was ever likely to need, given his reluctance to travel far. So he sat down with his father on one of the rare occasions when they were not surrounded by others and had a frank discussion.

It did not appertain to women, which removed a considerable potential for embarrassment from the two of them, nor THE subject, never to be discussed at all.

"Let's be sensible," said the elder Cosmo. "There's nothing there you particularly want to study, at least in a theoretical way." He cleared his throat.

"As far as I am aware, you want to be... ah... hands-on with all your interests, so why not go for something that might actually help the... ah... the Firm, the family business?"

Which is how the younger Cosmo got to read Computer Science and Philosophy at Oxford. Occasionally. But he was always aware, at the back of his mind, his father's words:

"Don't forget who you are and what you might yet be. Learning from experience is far more beneficial than from books, or even, from brilliant dons. Mine was one of the most exceptional Classicists of his day but he still took every possibility to disport himself at Parson's Pleasure by the river. You must have come across all that at the Dragon. Punting past when I was up just after the war and seeing wrinkly academics sunning themselves... ah... all over and making no attempt to cover their confusion is not a sight I shall forget in a hurry."

So Cosmo continued to go his own way, to get away when

he felt the need, which is how he had come to drive Route 66.

Reading 'Playboy'- and he did actually read the articles and short stories as well as grade the subjects of the photographs in a shorthand of his own, was a habit that he picked up while taking this extended vacation in the United States.

'Get your kicks on Route 66'- people had been singing it for nearly 25 years but it wasn't until the Rolling Stones recorded their version that Cosmo discovered a direction in Life, albeit only for a little while. The Rolling Stones, Mick in particular, had become something on an icon for the young man. While most of his contemporaries at Eton were mildly amused by the schism between AC/DC and Nirvana- 'mild amusement' being the height of any passion that they would admit to- he had always been a Stones' fan. He had even tried to get them to come and play at Mena Dhu, but no-one had ever heard of the place, especially not as a rock venue, so he had had to go to them. Imagine his delight upon finding a copy of their first album in a second hand bin in a large record store in Oxford Street, while his copy of 'Sticky Fingers' is still one of his prized possessions; he knew of no young lady, be it visiting Aristocrat, local County or resident maid, who could resist lowering the zip.

But now he had a watchword, a battle cry which, although he kept it to himself, drove him on.

Until that day when his tutor suggested that he take as long a sabbatical as he liked and come back when, or if he liked, when he withdrew several hundred dollars from one of his accounts and sent a telegram to his father- Lord Cosmo not being a fan of the telephone- saying; "Gone to Chicago. Going to LA."

Following consultation with Cousin Philip who believed himself to be a car, Cosmo had bought a 1970s Ford Mustang Mach 1, assured that he would always be able to sell it, and as in the song, had driven through St Louis and Joplin, Missouri and decided that Oklahoma City, famed for its massive cattle markets was only described as being 'oh, so pretty' because it was an easy rhyme. The central states seemed to be endless and the more or less identical Howard-Johnson motels, did nothing to change this impression. The trip only took two weeks and there were incontestable high spots but the nearer he got to all the modernity of the Pacific coast, the more he longed for his ancient house on the edge of the Atlantic. He came home.

Chapter Four

In the bar of *The de Coverlet Arms*, the ancient quayside inn in Porthwallow, the locals were having the perennial discussion about eligibility for the village cricket team for the annual end-of-season match to be held between Mena Dhu and Porthwallow. They were using the excuse of selecting the team to have an evening in the pub. It was an eclectic few: Charlie the Landlord, Jago Hocking and Hezekiah Pemberthy, occasional fishermen and jobbing builders and Nathan Treglown, their labourer.

In a few weeks' time, the annual match against the Big House would take place, one of the rare occasions when parts of the grounds were open to the public. There was a time when each player used to be allocated a number of tickets to distribute as they wish to provide local support and an appreciative gathering for Cook's legendary match teas. There were stories of sums in the hundreds of pounds being exchanged for one of these tickets and with it, a rare chance to visit the House. Subsequently, strangers with nothing to do with either side had been found wandering the corridors of Mena Dhu, amazed by what they saw. However, after the occasion when a lady scholar from Exeter University had been caught in the Nursery by the then Nurse, Maire O'Callaghan who, being Irish and much preferring hurling to cricket, had offered to sit with his Lordship and had physically kicked the interloper all the way down the drive, the remains of her folding Brownie, films fully exposed, stuffed up her walking shorts, they had decided to employ security to ensure it did not happen again and invite them all. Anyway, most in the village would have given their false teeth for a chance to see Mena Dhu.

Although not as old as the Big House, *The de Coverlet Arms* had been there in some form or other for more than 500 years and some of the wits of the village claimed that Charlie, the old landlord and Doris his wife had been there for most of them. Twenty five years ago, they had bought some of the old pilchard net sheds next door- sign of the decline in fishing- in which to house kitchens, which meant that things could change from it just being a beer shop to an eatery of note which only just managed to avoid the epithet of 'gastropub' by Charlie's curmudgeonly nature which he would assume as soon as any visitor compared the place with anywhere near London. Normally he had a twinkle in his eye and a well-intentioned insult on his lips, softened by a girlish giggle.

At the head of the table, as so often, was Jago Hocking, boatman, builder and general live wire. They were discussing team selection.

"What about Michael?" Jago suggested.

There was no denying it, nor would he try, even at forty something, Jago was star-struck. He had been in his late twenties when, like the rest of the world, he had first become aware of Michael, from off the albums and on the telly. But when, in fact, Michael Donohoe, the lead singer of *Michael and the Angels*, one of the finest Rock bands of the end of the twentieth century, had chosen to actually come and live in their village, in the Garden House after his wife had died, with their only son, Jake, and a housekeeper, his cup was over-flowing and when Michael had thrown himself, and his band totally into the escapade that had raised the money needed to rebuild the Village Hall, Jago, normally a phlegmatic type, was positively gushing about his new neighbour.

"If 'e'll play, 'e's in. Do they the world a good to be involved in sommat so traditional."

"D'you think 'e would?" asked Nathan, the big labourer. Rugby was really his game, but he could match any local blacksmith when it came to the smiting and flinging stakes of the country's summer game.

"Yeah- why not? All they pop stars is keen on cricket. Just think of Jagger," said Jago, "Matey got 'is own box at Lord's!"

"Bollocks!" said H.

Hezekiah Pemberthy or H. as he was widely known, despite a Methodist upbringing, or perhaps because of it, was as famous for his foul language as he was for his basic building techniques, but since he had got to know the Vicar during their performance of the Mechanicals' play from 'A Midsummer Night's Dream,' he had made some attempt at curbing his tongue.

"Ais. Tis a fact. Mick Jagger 'as a box at Lord's!"

"What...?"

And you could see H.'s brain working.

" Like... 'anging on the wall in the changing room? With 'is name writ inside?"

"What you on about?" asked Jago. Then the penny dropped. "Not 'is box- box, fer protecting those precious knackers- God, just imagine what they'd be worth if 'e 'd 'ave stood at stud! Not a cricket box but a box fer sittin' down in and watchin' the cricket from! You know, champagne and caviar, smoked salmon, prawn sandwiches; exchangin' *bon-mots* with Stephen Fry and Henry Blofeld. No, loads a they rock legends like their cricket. I bet Michael'd play."

"Well, best ask 'en." said H.

"I will- how about you askin' the Vicar?"

"'E never played before."

"We never asked him before."

"It'd mean the two of 'en. Can't imagine one without t'other."

They were referring to the Reverend Trevor Uphill who, despite having been the parish priest for twenty years, had only recently become accepted by the real local locals, few of whom actually went to church.

If they admitted to any faith, they would answer: Methodist; however, the Methodist chapel had been sold for second home holiday flats some twenty years before. The 'Methodies' had struggled along, with a sequence of sincere but seriously underpaid ministers who had been the first to attempt the multi-parish task, with one priest trying to minister to five or six parishes, but the mileage of a Sunday had become ridiculous. Eventually they had to give in and become 'ecumenical' which really had meant the death of the sect. Some of the elderly of the parish never set foot again in a church after the Chapel was sold.

Backalong, however, in the 1750s, as yet another example of their bloody-mindedness, the Cornish were retreating from the Church of England in droves. Despite having some of the finest churches in the country, the miners, farm labourers and fishermen preferred to gather together in the open air, bellow tuneful hymns and hear the Word from the Wesley Brothers.

They may well sound like some 50's pop combo, and in a way they were. They toured the country, in coaches on dreadful rutted roads through the wind and rain of the Cornish winters. When they could not get a carriage, they'd take a horse and if the horse was not forthcoming, they'd walk. But they'd get there. While Anglican clergymen were paying surrogate inferiors to serve in their draughty churches way out West while they themselves stayed in London or whichever of their parishes provided the most comfortable of livings, John Wesley in particular toured the whole country. One of their favourite venues was Gwennap Pit in Southern Cornwall, essentially a great inverted cone-shaped hole dug in the ground which he visited 18 times in his ministry. However, the places where they gathered were not always so salubrious. One meeting in an upper room in Polperro had to be abandoned because of the smell when it was discovered that it was above a fish cellar, filled with rotting conger eel.

Fortunately, Trevor had none of these problems, as the church of St Wallow was one of the jewels in a very fine local collection. Sadly, there was virtually no-one to appreciate it of a Sunday, except for old ladies, cramming for their finals. However, Trevor's break-through was due to the fact that he had lent the back of the church to the workmen when they needed a space to rehearse their play and then cemented his solidarity by acting the role of Peter Quince on the night.

The emergency provided by the landslide and destruction of the Village Hall the year before had re-vitalised Trevor and with him, almost inevitably, Jeremy Simmonds, his partner of more than the twenty years that he had been in Porthwallow. This gentle soul was invaluable to Trevor's life in many ways, most of them being secretarial. He was slight and trim, with a shy smile while the vicar was wiry and unkempt. As the selection committee sat in the pub, it was not impossible to imagine the pair of them fielding together at first and second slip or fighting a doughty rear-guard at numbers eight and nine in the batting order, so Jago pencilled in their names.

When Jago bumped into the Vicar and proposed the cricket match, Trevor was delighted. He himself was not much of an athlete but he knew that Jeremy was something of a dark horse on the cricket field, as he was most other places and while he would never put himself forward, would love to play, if asked.

Trevor had never really been sure at all about who he was.

After an average 2.2 in Classics from a minor Oxford College, the teaching world had been his only option and a job in Droitwich was better than no job at all. But occasional intimate skirmishes with members of both sexes amongst his colleagues had all proved pretty non-committal and fairly unexciting and it was this loneliness which had driven him to that fateful folk club where the music was painful, the coffee dire and the clients troglodytic. All except Jeremy.

As their tentative relationship flourished, his life at school declined and it was when a teen-aged girl had first of all asked him what the fuck use was Latin and then told him to: "Get a life, Mr Uphill" that he had handed in his notice and applied for training for the priesthood with the Church of England.

His four-year curacy had been purgatory in an inner-city parish in Birmingham, partially because he and Jeremy were not allowed to share the curate's digs and single bed, and partially because, for what was supposed to be a multi-cultural society, he had never met a more bigoted bunch, irrespective of race or colour.

When a perceptive bishop, at one of his regular little chats, had offered him Porthwallow- "and probably two or three other little churches- lovely buildings- very popular with weddings- the old codger they've got there is on his way out, thank the Lord- no, I mean that in a caring way- ", he had jumped at it and gradually the village had come to accept him and Jeremy for who they were: a loving couple, far happier than a number of those confined to so-called orthodox relationships in the place.

So Trevor and Jeremy were added to the list.

Then, from behind the bar: "I can play!"

"I bet she can an' all" replied H. under his breath.

The voice had come from Tegan.

Arguably the most beautiful young woman in the village, if not the whole of East Cornwall, Tegan Trembath, in her early twenties, stood five foot ten, witness to a drop of good English blood a few generations back, with a dark lambent colouring, witness to more than just a drop of Spanish blood from the exhausted survivors of the Spanish Armada who, having been harried all round the British Isles by bad weather and occasionally by the English navy, had managed to survive shipwreck off Land's End, swim ashore and cajole and charm their ways into welcoming Cornish beds. She had earned a place at university, had been to the big city, but unlike almost all of her contemporaries, had hated the false hedonism and naive politics of the place, had longed for, and had returned to the simpler struggle for existence back in her native village. Any man in the village with 20-20 vision and normal levels of testosterone would have happily wedded and bedded her, not necessarily in that order, but she had not yet met the one with whom she would spend the rest of her life. The nearest was Bobby, one of the grandsons of Admiral Hawkins who had moved to live in the village full-time after retiring from the

Navy; Bobby, named after his grandfather, was staying with him on an apparently permanent basis, providing Tegan with athletic sexual satisfaction when desired and his grandfather with care of a more general nature on a more regular basis.

"I used to play a bit when I was younger. At school and then at uni but, well, to be quite honest, there wasn't much of a Cornish women's league when I came back. I tried the local men's team but, sadly, as you can imagine, cricket wasn't what they almost all wanted to play with me. And there was never a ladies loo, not to mention a changing room at any of the grounds- too much hassle. I was even told to stick behind the bar and help serve the teas. He wasn't wearing his box at the time, that one, and should have been!"

"So," said Jago, consulting the scrap of paper filled with scrawl; "There's you, Hezekiah, me, Nathan, Steve, he'll 'ave to take a day off his harvesting-"

"If he ain't got it in by then, won't be worth harvestin'," added H., helpfully.

"Tegan, Bobby'll be playin' fer the Big House. I 'spect?"

"And Bobby must have played cricket. They sent him to that public school, after all."

"But 'e's one o' they" said H.

"I beg your pardon?!" Tegan retorted. "He is not!" The hint that Bobby, her current squeeze, might be queer was ridiculous.

"Naw," said H. "Not one o' they, like the Vicar, but one o' they, like, posh! Sir Cosmo'll 'ave signed 'im up already. Best be askin' Michael and the Vicar. Dun' ferget, tis Big 'Ouse versus Village. There's politics involved."

Time was, and that fairly recently, that the master of the Big House would simply contact old friends from Eton or Oxford or the Club and get a whole team down from I Zingari or the local MCC members and thrash whatever opposition the village had been able to offer. But someone, possibly a wife or sister, had pointed out that this rather smacked of Colonialism and the thing should be made up of locals on both sides. Hence the selection meetings.

Up at the Big House, the same subject was under discussion.

"You'd best get the Admiral's boy, straight away, before he's inveigled away by that splendid creature. No man could refuse her anything," said Cosmo.

"Tegan?" replied the butler.

"Absolutely. I seem to remember he got a hundred at Lord's, the Eton-Harrow game. No-one else will know that, as nobody else I know in the village reads 'the Times', certainly not the cricket pages, certainly not since poor old CMJ passed over, and the lad's not the type to boast." said Sir Cosmo. "His granddad did mention it, but he was in the Navy and I don't think fully understands such matters."

Hives rang later that morning and Bobby was flattered.

"I did bring my coffin, just in case"

"Isn't that rather pessimistic, sir?"

"No, Hives. It's what we call the bag we carry all our cricket gear around in these days. So much more that when it was just a box, a cap and a bat. What with helmets and pads and thigh pads and what-have-you?"

"Then you'll play for the House?"

"I'd love to- I'll have to bring Pops, if that's ok?"

"I'm sure Sir Cosmo would be delighted to welcome Sir Robert. Is he up to umpiring?"

"Not really. I don't think his bladder would last that long. But he might score."

"The boys reckon you'll play for the Big House?"

Tegan was lying on top of Bobby, subsequent to an afternoon's gentle sex.

"Well, Mister Hives did ring- yes..."

"Did you play at school?"

"Well, yes, actually. It was about the only thing I was any good at."

"Yes- I suppose there isn't a section on your end of term report for sexual invention and endurance."

"Surprisingly, no. What mark would you have given?" And he squirmed under her a bit.

"Six out of ten. Could do better."

"Then I'd better practise!"

"Can I play?!"

"Jake!"

"Sorry-"

Michael O' Donohue's son, Jake, now nearly nine, was at the end of his first year at the Porthwallow Academy, as the Primary School had come to be known a few years previously. The theory was that by changing the name on the jar, rather than improving upon the contents, the end-product was magically going to get better. In the end, common sense prevailed and they simply lowered the bar to produce the never-ending climb of the success graphs much loved of London-based administrators. And if they could have a pi-chart or two, so much the better.

Prior to that, what education Jake had received had come from his father and mother, often backstage before the evening's arena performances. When she had died, the place of his mother, at least in the education stakes, had been taken by a magnificent lady whose every deed only went to show why the English produce the best nannies.

But this year, as Michael felt at home at last, partly because he and the young teacher, Sandy, had become an item, Jake was settled into the local school. He was streets ahead of almost all the other 40 children which, in a different child, could have been a recipe for anarchy. Instead, he had become a mixture of teaching assistant and teaching aid, having been to almost everywhere they came across in Geography and having a phenomenal brain for mathematics. He was quite remarkable except for the fact that he would insist on calling the subject 'Math', rather than 'Maths' having first learned the rudiments in the States from his mother, in the back of the tour bus, which was why his father refused to correct him.

The only sad moment recently was when Mrs Gilchrist, for so long Jake's nanny-cum-tutor, had handed in her resignation.

"I'm very sorry, Michael, but I've got to go."

"But, Mrs G."

"No, please don't try to persuade me or I'll cry and I had promised myself that I wouldn't. You don't need me; you've got Sandy and she's catering for you in ways that I never could. Or at least, was not employed for. And Jake is at school which is at least not holding him back. I'm wasting my time and your money-"

"Oh, blow the money-"

"Easy to say for those as has it. But when you've been poor, it does become important. I shan't be poor again, thanks to you but I need a new challenge. I've contacted Little Ones, asked to be put back on their books."

"Are you sure?"

"Absolutely."

"And is there anything you need?"

"Well, if you would write a reference...?"

Michael was trying to be firm and reasonable with his son.

"I don't expect any other children will be playing-"

"They don't know how- they all play soccer- even the girls!" said Jake.

"Well, you don't know how either," said his father.

"Yeah, maybe but I played Little League baseball in the

States- it can't be very much different."

"Don't you let any real cricketers hear you say that."

"But can I play, Pop- er- Dad? Can I?"

"We'll have to wait and see." And then Jake switched approach.

"Are you gonna play?"

"We'll just have to wait and see."

When the invitations came by way of embarrassed 'phone calls from Jago (he was deemed to be the better acquainted with both on account of having served on the Village Hall Rescue Committee with them) both couples, the Vicar and Jeremy, and Michael and his son leapt at the opportunity. Beneath it all, being asked to play cricket for the village is what every Englishman and, more and more, every English woman, desires. When Michael told Sandy, his 'girlfriend' was very quiet until Jake, in a moment of childish insight, asked: "But don't you wanna play, too?" and she could not deny that she would rather like to, if there was room.

"Wanna get me to teach you how to play?" asked Jake but Sandy quietly refused and said; "Actually I might be able to show you a thing or two," whereupon violent and hysterical practice sessions took place in secret behind the high walls of the Garden House, Sandy revealing remarkable ability at off-spin bowling.

Chapter Five

'Middle-aged minor aristocrat living far from London seeks wife. No gold-diggers, women's liberationists nor anyone under 25 need apply.' "There. What do you think?" Cosmo had been at his desk, slaving over the wording of the advertisement for hours. His rolled gold Mont Blanc fountain pen was blotted with ink, as were both his hands- he had something of an accident while refilling it- while the paper in front of him was more crossings-out than legible words.

"Hives," he called to the butler who had popped his head around the accounts' room door to enquire after developments. "What this needs is a woman's point of view. Would you mind awfully asking Mrs Walker to pop in?"

Mr Hives approached the desk and pressed a switch on the ancient intercom which, elsewhere would have been consigned to a museum, or a skip, but which in Mena Dhu acted as the hub of communications. at least on behalf of young Sir Cosmo. Other, more normal people use mobile phones, but his Lordship was certain that they did things to your brains and so refused to even learn how to use them.

"They all turn themselves off as soon as I press anything. What good is that?"

"Edie?" Mr Hives was summoning the house keeper.

"Aye, aye?" came a crackling voice.

"Could you step along to the Counting House? His Lordship would welcome the benefit of your gender."

Mrs Walker popped her rubicund face around the massive door.

"You need a woman, my lord?" she said, jokingly.

"As a matter of fact, I do- or rather, a wife, which isn't necessarily the same thing, I mean, of course, all wives are women, but not all women wives, if you see what I mean? I'm going to advertise."

"On the television?" she asked, mock-seriously.

"Oh, do you think so? I hadn't thought of that." And he looked critically at a reflection of himself in the mirror over the granite fireplace. What he saw rather pleased him; maroon cords, an orange-coloured fisherman's smock which he had had made specially for him on the Isles of Scilly, greying locks reminiscent of Oscar Wilde, a short beard, the style of which suited him better than it had James the First, and his smoking cap which was a most beautiful, deep vermilion velvet. He also wore, at his throat, a red, spotted item which he refused to call a cravat and referred to as a bandana. He never wore shoes indoors.

"No," he said. "I had thought more of a little something in 'The Lady'"

"Let's have a look." She shimmied across to the desk, attracting Sir Cosmo's attention.

"I don't suppose...?"

"Far too old, my lord. And I'm happy as I am." She smiled winningly at Hives, who actually blushed. "Though 'tis kind of you to consider it."

"Oh, I do," said Cosmo. "I do. Often."

"Now," said Mrs Walker, picking up the bi-focals which hung from the pink diamante chain around her neck.

"'Middle-aged minor aristocrat'? Hmm, there is this rather annoying euphemism for 'second-hand' going about these days and that's 'previously loved'; do you think we could find something along those lines instead of 'middle-aged?"

"Well, not 'previously loved' because that's the whole point. And I am, damn it! Middle-aged, that is. And even that is being a bit economical. I mean, double forty-eight and you get to be ninety-six and I have no intention of living that long. Although, if you look at the Pater, he could go on for ever, as long as there's somebody to change his bottle."

Mrs Walker looked sympathetic.

"Oh, my lord. You don't want to be thinking that way- after all, the whole point of the exercise is for you to father an heir and you must think young thoughts for such things."

"I don't know; there's girls in the village who no sooner look at a male over twelve and they book a place in that maternity suite for years on end, it seems, while there's others, only one or two mind, who could match the Trinidadian guppy for partners and still get nowhere." Exotic fish was one of Cosmo de Coverlet's many interests.

"How about 'mature'!?

"Do you think so? I'm sure Hives doesn't agree."

"My lord, from the little I know about the advertising industry, hyperbole is a *lingua franca*."

"All right. So. 'Mature'. 'Minor aristocrat'?"

"Again, my lord," said Edith, "you mustn't run yourself down. There's nothing minor about the family estates, as far as I am aware."

"Well, no- Auntie Bettie's boy's big round here but I think I am number two. Or three, if you take in the National Trust. But we own bits right across country as far as John O'Groats. In fact, I might even own that, as well."

"So. 'Wide-spread?' Living far from London-"

"Oh, yes. Anyone who wants a... a metrocentric existence is a definite no-no. Can't stand the place. Fortunately, Father is still officially the holder of the seat in the House of Lords, so I'm safe there. Don't have to go. Even when whipped."

"So, rural, possibly?!

"Absolutely."

"Now- 'seeks wife'". Mrs Walker looked at him over the glasses in a mock-stern manner.

"If you don't mind me saying so, my lord, you do rather make is sound like a children's party game- a cross between Hide and Seek and Kiss in the Ring."

"Be rather fun, what? Mrs Walker, I think you may have hit on the answer- ask a few fillies down, distant rellies, the odd duke's younger daughter, that sort of thing, get a few crates of the '88 up- not the '90- that would be overdoing it but something nice and then, Spin the Bottle."

"I still think a discrete advertisement in 'the Lady' would be a starter."

"Oh, all right. Pity."

On the morning after the next week's publication of 'the Lady', there was a telephone call to the Big House, early.

"Mena Dhu?"

"That you, Mr 'Ives?"

Even in his pyjamas, patent leather slippers and silk dressing gown, Hives was immaculately well spoken.

"Indeed, and to whom am I speaking?"

"It's Bruce Jones, St Austell Sorting Office."

"Sorting what?"

"Royal Mail. Look, Mr 'Ives, we gotta sort of a problem."

"And how can we help?"

"Well. it's your mail, Mr 'Ives." The voice down the lines sounded frazzled, even at such an early hour.

"Can't your man, Alistair, handle it? He's normally excellent. He's got a van, hasn't he? I know he's most conscientious with the gates."

"Well, the thing is, you see, is the volume. We can't get them all in the one van. So I was wondering, would it be alright if he brings the first half dozen up this morning, and the next lot tomorrow. I doubt you'll get through them all in one day."

It took all week.

Sir Cosmo was not allowed to look at the photographs,

some of which could have been used in a basic gynaecology text book. Mrs Walker monitored those and only allowed the fully clad; Hives rejected any with an excessive number of spelling or grammatical errors or who addressed their letter: "Hi!"

A sound basic education was essential. Sir Cosmo scanned them for length, either excessive or inadequate, on the grounds that it may reflect the author exactly or inversely- four pages of hand-written A4 and she would be as reticent as a mouse, while a few terse lines, telegram-style, might hold back a tsunami of exposure *viva voce*. Even so, there were hundreds to be considered: the egocentric who sent CVs and covering letters, beginning 'I'; the provocative 'I don't know who you are but you sound divine!' often in a turquoise ink, and the 'you really need to see me to appreciate me' type, who terrified his lordship.

In the end, he turned them all down and went to Newquay for the week-end.

On Cosmo's return from Newquay, and whatever attractions, unimaginable to Hives, had drawn him there, he raised the subject again.

"You see," he started, as though the conversation had not discontinued, "What I suddenly realised was that, if I don't squeeze out a sprog before I pop off, well- I don't quite know how to tell you this but, put simply, cousin Philip would be the next in line." This came as such a shock that Hives, normally so self-possessed, actually sat down without invitation.

"Surely not? There must be..."

"This is it, you see, my dear Hives. As the ineffable Mick Jagger once wrote: 'You can't always get what you want'".

Hives' anxiety must be explained.

Philip de Coverlet, Cosmo's cousin, arguably the next in line, thought of himself as a car. Almost always had done, ever since Noddy's little red motor had come into his life, going 'parp, parp, parp' all those years ago and taken it over. So he had been a Morris Minor when young, with a red soft top and white sides, and he too went 'parp, parp' and, once he had learned the proper way to do it, drove himself around the house and the estate at Mena Dhu, all the while producing a running commentary.

"I am slowing down. I am stopping. I am putting on the hand brake and switching off the ignition."

Often behind the sofa in the main sitting room.

They thought he would grow out of it but instead he simply became more and more prestigious cars. When he first saw the James Bond films, he was an Aston Martin with a throaty roar for a while but he did not enjoy it; he never got anywhere with girls, anyway. So he reverted to being whichever of the fleet of ageing Rolls Royces that sat in the stables at Uncle Cosmo's old house that currently took his fancy.

A progressive (and very expensive) preparatory school had agreed to take him and even to allow him to call his study-bed room 'the garage'. The fact that little Philip sat motionless and passive throughout lessons and only came to life when they allowed him to switch on his ignition at the end did not seem to faze any of the young teachers.

He passed Common Entrance with flying colours, much to everyone's surprise, despite the assertion from the Head that it was never in any doubt. Eton forced him to be a little more 'normal' because some teachers, the scientists in particular, would take off House Points for misbehaviour and the House Prefects would see to it that Philip stopped.

"How can it be 'misbehaviour'?" argued a more pedantic prefect. "He isn't behaving at all!"

It had been hoped that he would join the steady if irregular procession of de Coverlets to Christchurch College, Oxford but he was being a particularly precious Hispano-Suiza with the roof down on the day of the interview and the dons who followed in the footsteps of Charles Ludwig Dodson turned this eccentric down.

Cambridge didn't, and it had been at Cambridge that a certain don who thought he recognised genius when he saw it, tapped him on the shoulder one day and invited him to join the Foreign Office.

Fortunately, and despite appearances, there are some very intelligent gentlemen running the Foreign Office- not the politicians, of course; they come and go with boring regularity and are saved from 'cocking the whole show up' as the Permanent Under-Secretary of State for Foreign Affairs put it over a stiff mineral water at his club, by the civil servants.

There was a distant sort of relative of the de Coverlets in amongst them, fortunately far enough from the main stock and branch to have his idiosyncrasies restricted to the wearing of Hush Puppies, and he kept an eye on Philip, managing to move him on ahead of any disaster that he might have caused coming to light.

Resulting from a representative of Her Majesty's Government, namely Philip, being involved in the smuggling of cocaine from the steamy activity of Bogota as his part in the funding of the reconstruction of the Porthwallow Village hall, it had been deemed suitable that somewhere cool and almost inert might be best for his next posting and Ulaan Bataar seemed ideal.

"Ulaan Bataar!" he said to cousin Cosmo when last he had come to stay at Mena Dhu. "I mean, Christ, Cuzzers! End of the world, almost. Don't have any cars at all, hardly. They actually tow theirs around by horse!"

But he had promised to come down for the cricket match if he hadn't had to leave for Mongolia before.

"Well, then," said Mrs Walker, "how about inviting them down here?"

"Rather like the Hunt Ball," suggested Hives, "but more refined? Fewer young farmers. We could invite the rugby team instead."

"I wouldn't have to go anywhere? They'd come to me? Now that is worth thinking about."

Chapter 6

Jago and Hezekiah worked together and had done so for so long that the one augmented the other. H. had played rugby for Cornwall when it was not the refined game it is now. Stories of his achievements in the depths of the loose scrums down in Hellfire Corner in Redruth are still whispered in awe among Trelawney's Army. But he drinks little now and is happily married.

For Jago, that will never be.

The travel bug had bitten Jago Hocking while still young; in his early twenties he had already been round the world and back again, away for several years. But before that, he had had a true epiphany, on a number of levels.

Soon after leaving school, he had got a job as a deck hand on a boat, the *Mighty Albion*, out of Mevagissey, just along the coast. The skipper, Albert Dingle, if he was in a good mood, would occasionally let him steer and would teach him the rudiments of astral navigation.

"But, Bert," Jago had said, "Us can always switch on the GPS".

The old man spat. "Not if 'n tis fucked. Tis the same as sex, boy, you gotta learn how to do it without all they mechanical toys!"

But Jago was essentially a deck hand, working with rod and line and gutting the catch. That summer, it was better than gold mining because shoals of tuna had somehow found their ways up from Spanish waters into the Western Approaches and the Cornish boats were busy, heaving them out of the sea on pole and line.

The Mighty Albion was full to bursting and so Bert decided to take her into Roscoff, on the north coast of Brittany, to unload.

"You can go ashore," he said to his crew of three- Jago and two older men who tended to do as they were told, "But we'm sailin' at five-You in't on board, you'm walkin' ome! And a word of warning, young Jago- their cider tastes like fruit juice but kicks like Bobby Charlton. And stay away from the local brandy- Calvados, they do call it".

But of course, Jago did not listen to the words of the wise and after several pints of their subtle cider, couldn't remember the name of what he wasn't to drink, chased it with several glasses of Calvados and so, as the *Mighty Albion* steamed out of Roscoff, past the Ile de Batz, Jago Hocking was fast asleep on the beach in a pool of his own vomit.

He went for a swim, fully clothed, counting on the morning sun to dry him off and then went looking, first for breakfast and secondly for help. The first was not possible, because he found that he had drunk what little money he had had and could not even afford a waffle, another of the region's specialities, and so shambled in to the Office de Tourisme de Roscoff. A prim, slim middle-aged lady with a nose as sharp as a quill looked down it at Jago.

"*Oui?*" She managed to ask and sniff at the same time.

"You- Spick- English?" asked Jago in his worst display of an Englishman abroad. This time, the sniff came before the reply. "If I 'ave to."

This annoyed Jago. "'ow about- *'A wodhes'ta kewsel Kernewek?'*" (for the few of my readers who do not immediately understand the Cornish, this means: 'Do you speak Cornish?').

It was all the Cornish Jago knew but enough to rebuff the ruder visitors who tried to make fun of the local accent; however, on old pen features, it had the most surprised and surprising effect. Her face lit up.

"Da! A little." And she rattled off something in Breton that Jago could not understand.

"I'm sorry- that was a bit fast. Can we use English?"

"If we 'ave to." The sniff was back but Jago's origins had completely changed her attitude.

She found some acceptable clothing in the town lost-and-found department- obviously, a lot of people were no longer interested in finding what they had lost- and although the gaudy Hawaian shirt might have looked out of place elsewhere, in a Breton holiday resort, it passed; the habit of wearing long baggy shorts, adopted from American basketball players and imported around the world by their fans was something of a handicap for Jago, who was not tall and had they been a few inches longer, he would have tripped over the turn-ups. As it was, he had to rescue his stout leather belt from the shambles that had been his own clothing in order to keep his new shorts up. Unsurprisingly, there was no underwear amongst the second-hand clothing, except for a dubious pair of pink knickers, which would have to do. Flip-flops, the common footwear of almost everyone in Roscoff rounded off his 'ensemble' and fortunately, there was no mirror in the Office de Tourisme clothes store. As he had changed, his deliverer had surreptitiously kept glancing at her charge and, a woman at heart, had appreciated what she saw.

"And now?"

"Well, I could murder a bacon buttie and a cup of tea."

"Murder?!"

"I 'spect tis different in Cornish."

After he had had a bowl of coffee and half a *baguette*, he felt a better man. He was even enjoying his underwear.

"Now" said Minette, as his deliverer was called, "Money. We can lend you ze fare so that you can return..."

"Tis kind but, thing is, I ain't got money at 'ome. I spent me last sou last night. I'd need a proper job to pay me way. Do any of the boats need a 'and?"

"I think not- they are all at sea- when there are so many *'ton'*- er- tuna, everyone wants a part. And we are in the middle of onion time-"

Jago looked at her, wondering if she had translated correctly.

"The harvest of the onions. *Chez nous*, we are famous for

our pink onions- *un petit moment-*" And she reached for a phone, checked a number on her Filofax and rang someone.

"Monsieur le Compte, s'il vous plait..." She cupped her hand over the receiver. "A local business. He might need a 'and." And when the other end returned she fired off in such a rattle of incomprehensible discourse that Jago did not know whether it was Breton or French that she was using. Eventually, she rang off and smiled at Jago.

"*Eh, ben-oui!!* All the 'elp they can get. And it's not far."

Minette took him out of the office and pointed out the road he was to take, out of town to the south west. Jago thanked her profusely but it seemed that at least some of the pleasure had been hers for, as he turned to walk away, she squeezed his bum appreciatively.

The fields of sandy rows, to all appearances a gritty wasteland apart from what seemed to be the dead leaves of some plant, started quite near to the town and Jago was initially dispirited at the prospect. But then, he noticed something remarkable: what seemed to be a pair of legs, standing on their own, the feet in a pair of what he discovered later to be clogs, '*sabots*', great hunks of wood roughly cut to fit almost any foot, especially when the owner afforded themselves the luxury of a pair of felt slippers that went inside. However, from these clogs, two statuesque, naked legs rose; they might have rung a distant bell had Jago spent more attention in the one English class when the teacher had indulged himself in a favourite poem:

Ozymandias, although these were not legs of stone. They were most definite flesh, beautifully bronzed flesh, terminating in a pair of ragged, very short denim shorts. It took Jago a while to realise that the owner of these legs was in fact bent double, picking onions. It was when she stood up that the magnificence of the vision was complete. Around a gently sweating body was tied a work-shirt, knotted at the slender waist, while her hair- Jago had confirmed most definitely that it was a female figure- was engulfed in an old floppy sunhat. He approached, mesmerised; the girl- for she was still young enough to be called a girl- stood watching. The nearer he got, the easier he could see the smile, slowly spreading across her tanned and sweaty face.

"*Ici? Pour les oignons?*" he asked.

"*Ah,ban-oui.* I 'ope so. Ozzerwise I am wasting my time, busting my butt if zey are not onions." The American slang sounded strange on her very French lips. "An' you are the *pauvre pecheur?* Ze inebriated fisher?"

Jago had reluctantly admitted that it was so, ashamed of having to admit his petty follies to such a goddess.

"I am glad- ozzerwise I should be frightened of such a man in such clothes!"

"They'm better that the ones I left behind" returned Jago, determined not to be phased by the fact that all his senses were on automatic pilot and that on red alert. She was gorgeous!

"Come, little man-" she said, obviously used to being obeyed. Normally, Jago objected to references to his height, just under five foot eight inches, but even without clogs, she must have stood at six foot. "I am Nicole". And she turned- which in itself played havoc with his baser instincts- and he had to try to think of anything- cold porridge, lugworms, stewed prunes- anything to keep his mind (and those parts of his body which were reacting independent of his thought processes) away from the bottom in front. She led him to a shed at the edge of the field in which some basic tools of the hoeing variety were kept along with various sun-bleached pairs of bib and braces-style dungarees. She turned and looked at him up and down, obviously calculating his height with a look that showed that it was something that she did often and not only a man's height that she judged this way.

"Take'em off, zen, big boy."

"Wha-?"

"Unless you want to frighten ze seagulls- and zese *'bleus'* will be more *confortable*. Don't be shy." And she stood there, his dungarees in her hand, weighing them slightly.

Jago was not a bashful fellow so he threw off the Hawaian shirt, quite proud of his torso, tanned and firm from landing tuna. He undid the belt but any attempt to control the removal of his baggy basketball shorts in an attempt to try to hide the obvious effect that girl was having on him failed as he fumbled and dropped them, revealing his previously-loved underwear.

"Pink!? Ooh-la-la!" she crowed.

"They in't mine!" Jago tried but she wouldn't not hold back.

"That's what they all say! But... ah... no time for such matters- now. We 'ave to work."

And work they did. For the rest of the day, until both of them, hot and sweaty, returned to the shed.

"Now..." she said and wiped the sweat that was slowly trickling from the bottom of her neck down into the folds of her sweat-soaked work shirt.

"Right!" said Jago, misunderstanding her intentionally. He loosened his belt, whereby the wet dungarees slipped of their own accord off his shoulders. This left him virtually naked, apart from the pink panties and they did not last long, as her shirt had somehow become unknotted, revealing what he had suspected all along, that she forswore underwear. The old little denim shorts went the way of all cloth and soon they discovered that they were made for each other. Several times.

Eventually, when it was beginning to get dark, which it did quite late in summer in Roscoff, and they could hear the maid calling them to supper, they lay back, side by side and she said; "*Eh bien*. So! It is not true what they say about ze English."

"I ain't English. I'm Cornish."

"Makes all ze diff'rence, obviously. You can stay until you 'ave earned your ticket 'ome."

"May take some time."

Jago stayed all summer.

When lying quietly in the little room that they had found him in the chateau conveniently near to Nicole's, he contemplated becoming an onion farmer, with such a wife and such a house but his dreams were shattered when he asked: "Shall I come back next year? Pick some more?", only to be told that she would not be there. This summer was really only a break at home in her career as a dancer.

"*Exotique,*" she explained.

"D'you mean 'stripper'!?" Jago asked, only to have his testicles squeezed none too gently as she reacted angrily. "*Non!* At the Folies, we start naked!"

Apparently she danced in the chorus at the famous nightclub in Paris, and all the onion-picking had done wonders for her waistline which was not exactly a six-pack but certainly as firm and as round as a cider jar.

It had been this whole adventure that had started Jago wondering and then wandering, all round the world and back again and this contact that had directed Nicole's father, M. le compte de Briand, in his better-known persona of Onion Johnny, to Porthwallow and subsequently Mena Dhu whenever the Bretons came over with their onions. On rare occasions, Nicole had come with her '*papa*' and the reunions had been memorable.

It had been the sight of Nicole in not very much during one of her visits that had inspired Tegan, then a string bean of a thirteen-year-old, to make something of herself. She used to slouch around the village, as if apologising for her very existence and Nicole had noticed.

"Why don't you stand up, *cherie?*", she asked whereupon she herself stretched her full six feet and projected her chest, a sight punters paid hundreds of euros to see in Paris.

"But I've got nothing here," said Tegan, scratching at her vest.

"You will, darling, you will, and when you do, how do you say, flaunt it!"

That was a few years back.

Then, the previous year, at the great oak portal to the kitchen that was laughingly known as the Back Door, there was a knock. Such an event was rare, as visitors were passively discouraged. Nothing was done about the upkeep of the front gate and drive way up through the woods to the house so it was only the local delivery drivers, such as Alf the milkman and the butcher who also provided those fruits and vegetables that Abel and the boy did not grow somewhere around the estate, who would use it. Sir Cosmo had given a directive that none of the supermarket chains should be allowed, and no-one in Mena Dhu was particularly adept with computers for online shopping. Cook went to open it and was greeted by a waft of garlic and kisses on both cheeks by a parody of a Frenchman: black beret, blue and white striped top, a red neckerchief and wooden clogs. Leaning by the doorpost was an old sit-up-and-beg bicycle, the handlebars laden with strings on rosy onions.

"Cookie!"

"Johnnie!" cried the plump old woman and embraced him back. "I'll take whatever you've got!"

It was, of course, Onion Johnnie from Roscoff, less well known as le compte de Briand, Nicole's *papa*.

"Come in- come in- *entrez.*" Cook had just about exhausted her French vocabulary but the little man, an irregular visitor to

Mena Dhu, helped out. "I was going to see Jago?"

"I d'reckon 'e'll be out- there's mack'rel in the bay!" said the old cook.

"So I sink, instead: ah, Cookie! She will want onions-"

"If that's all you got," she said, pointing to all the strings of Roscoff onions handing from the handlebar of the old push bike of the even older man "we'll 'ave they all."

"You' re a wonder, Cookie- I have more in the van. And also..." And he pointed roughly in the direction of the front gate but had to look away, as tears blurred his vision.

Happily, the old woman did not notice.

"But you'll 'ave your tea an' a cream scone, first. Jago will want a chat, at least. An' you'm goin' no further tonight- even if we do 'ave to kidnap yer bike!"

The old Renault van, recently repainted in the *tricolores* and the *gwen-ha-du*, the black and white of Brittany, pulled up on the quay outside of *The Coverlet Arms*, parking right in front of the No Parking signs.

Tegan, who saw this through the window, gave a delighted cry: "Nicole!" but as she was bustling out from behind the bar, the figure who was framed in the doorway stopped her in her tracks. She was bald; gone was that glorious shining chestnut mane; the body that had for a while made her a considerable fortune had gone- victim to a double mastectomy and ineffective chemotherapy- so that what flesh was left hung from her frame and the immaculate make-up only masked a skull. True, it was dressed with much guile and expense by the best seamstresses of the Folies, but the only thing about her that Tegan recognised, once Nicole had removed her film-star dark glasses, were her eyes.

"Tegan, *cherie!*" The voice was huskier than unusual. "No, don't cry or you'll start me off and you cannot imagine how long I spent on my mascara." The two women stood in the middle of the empty pub, hugging each other and the pain grew in Tegan's face as she felt the extent of the ravages on the older woman's body.

"So!" came a cry from the door. "Where is she then? Where's my- oh , Christ!"

Jago had seen her.

"Hello, big boy." she tried their usual greeting, dating back to the onion fields of Roscoff but could not be brave any longer. He took her from the pub and put her in the van, drove out to the cliffs and there they spent the night, sitting in the van, holding hands, just talking in so far as she could still talk. In the morning, she left him there and drove back to the Big House to collect her father; Cosmo had been more than happy to offer him hospitality and a room in the West Wing when he heard the story as well as a pledge to buy as many pink onions as he could sell.

Jago stood and watched her go. They did not see each other again.

Chapter Seven

"The question is- or rather, the questions are- how and where might he meet someone... suitable."

The subject of Sir Cosmo's marriage was never far from the minds of the female staff.

It was at one of the Mena Dhu's spectacular staff breakfasts that Mrs Walker suddenly exclaimed:

"A Ball!"

Abel Tonkin, supposing that she, like him, was continually thinking of the cricket match, replied reassuringly: "Naw, dun you worry, misses; I got boxes o' balls as surprisingly went missing when I was working up Lunnon. Suitable for every wicket as I can prepare, one for us to bowl with, one fer the opposition; some o' they picked and scuffed by the finest cheats are ever played at Lord's. All's fair in love an' cricket."

It was the most he had said for years.

"Thank you, Abe, but I didn't mean cricket balls. Come on, Hives," she said to the butler who was finely filleting a nice kipper. "While the iron hot."

"Oh, no- surely not. Do I have to?"

Hives and Mrs Walker had hurried into Cosmo's smoking room where, as usual, he was prone on his relaxator, digesting.

"The best place to meet the finest crop of young ladies, they do say," said Mrs Walker.

"No! I was so pleased when Auntie Betty stopped those awful Queen Charlotte thrashes. Cousin Margaret said every tart in London use to get in- Uncle Philip said they were bloody silly. Too much temptation, if you ask me. I was horrified when they started them again, even without Her Maj. I was inveigled into taking a table. Never again. A couple of grand! I thought I was going to a party. Nobody told me I was supposed to bring a party."

It was back in about 2010 that the wives of those who believed themselves to be the great and the good had, over lunch in Le Gavroche, thought to resurrect the Queen Charlotte's Ball and somehow had sent an invitation to Mena Dhu. Nobody was really sure who lived there but word had it, in the corridors of No.11 Downing Street that, if his tax returns, whoever he may be, this de Coverlet, were anything to go by, then he must be worth inviting and the ladies suggested that he sponsor a table.

"I don't want a bloody table." he had said. "There'll only be me. I don't know anybody else. And if they really are aristocrats, I'm likely to be related to them all. Too much explanation. I doubt Auntie Betty would like me to go."

But he had gone. And caused a hoo-haa, though not the one he expected. He had had to open up the Grosvenor Square house, disturbing the Portuguese couple who looked after the place, when Cosmo and Hives, who had offered to act as chauffeur, came up the night before. Dressing had taken much of the day. On the few occasions that he was sent an official invitation that mentioned "white tie", or even 'black tie' for that matter, Cosmo had taken it in the way of the Highland lairds and used it as an opportunity to wear his full Cornish regalia. Resplendent in black and gold tartan, the kilt, the sporran and all the rest were a magnificent sight, even on one as insignificant as Cosmo; and when he added the insignia of some of the more obscure orders to which the family belonged, he positively glowed. And none of it imitation.

They were fortunate to have the underground garage in the square, so Hives could drive Sir Cosmo straight to the ball. The old Bentley had caused a stir through Mayfair but not as great a one as his Lordship descending the stairs into the ballroom itself. Intended as a flattering background against which the young girls in their virgin-white ball gowns could make their entrances, it was even better suited to the magnificence of Cosmo in his Cornish kilt.

At first, the hostesses, the matriarchs most determined to be rid of their daughters, had directed Security to 'bounce' this nutcase but he discretely displayed his ticket and explained who he was.

"Lord?!" the two ladies squeaked between themselves. "I thought de Coverlet was some sort of hedge fund!"

The quicker thinking of the two summoned the Maitre'd, who was being paid a vast sum to stage-manage such hiccups, and told him to show his Lordship to the de Coverlet table. Right at the centre of the room. Laid in exquisite crystal and silverware, ten places awaited him and a vast ice bucket with ten bottles of outrageously over-priced *methode-champagnoise* wine for starters.

Innumerable and interchangeable young girls, some pleasingly busty, others horribly thin *a la mode*, had processed past his table, some on the arms of their insistent mothers, the more adventurous alone; but almost all were fazed by his habit of addressing their chests, rather than their expensively made-up faces. As Cosmo knew nothing about the results at Henley or Wimbledon and very little about Lord's, had never heard of words like 'Wikileaks' and 'vuvuzela' and really only cared for the history and business affairs of his family, a total *terra incognitia* for even the brightest girl, conversations were stilted, to say the least. The only experience any of them had of Cornwall had been of vomiting horribly after a few days on real Scrumpy when they had been to Rock after their exams, something of a tribal migration among those of their ilk and none of the Porthwallow young people that Cosmo knew ever went to that kind of school.

Then the dancing started.

On reflection, Cosmo realised that asking the band for the Floral Dance was probably not a very good idea.

"You remember? Terry Wogan? It's very easy. One, two, three, hop- and that's about it." But sadly the Jive Aces were unfamiliar with the piece and so vowing never again, the Lord de Coverlet had left quite early.

Eventually, Cosmo gave into the pressure coming from below stairs.

"Could you look in to it? And come up with a guest list of the least objectionable of the applicants. And they must all live near enough to go home after. We're not having a house full of hoydens and harridans staying over for breakfast! And definitely not their mothers!"

The dozen or so invitations, sent to those ancient families which actually had a young girl of an even vaguely suitable age- anywhere between twenty and forty- were swiftly dispatched. Hives had discretely approached his counterparts among the households of the St Aubans, the Godolfins, the Bolithos and Carew Poles, the Rashleighs, Trefrys and Vivians, the Boscawens and Bassets among others to discover, not necessarily whether there was a suitable young lady looking for marriage but whether there were any girls who liked a bit of a knees-up and indeed, word came back that in fact there were some high-spirited gals, and those who were not on GAP years and were currently working as P.A.s in either advertising or TV, or running the equine departments of the family estates would be interested. There was even one enterprising noble young lady who had joined the current trend and had set up her own gin distillery which, coupled with the famous name of the family estates, was doing very well. She offered them an excellent deal on her product.

"Band or disco?"

It was the invariable question that arose whenever anyone was organising anything like this.

"Oh, in Heaven's name, not a disco."

It was his Lordship who voiced the thought going through the minds of all those on the organizing committee- himself, Hives, Mrs Walker and Cook.

"No debate?" asked Mrs Walker.

"Well, you can debate it as much as you like but we are not having anything like a discotheque at Mena Dhu. Over my dead body and it would probably kill Father as well. There are several excellent brass bands in the district, I believe."

"With the exception, sir, of the Floral dance, there are very few numbers in the brass band repertoire suitable for dancing."

"The Floral dance is about the only one I can do, so why should anyone want more? They did make us learn to waltz at Eton but those were encounters that I have consciously put out of my mind, along with the moves that went with them. I have no idea where they found the young ladies, but they put back my sexual development by several years. Anyway, there are some pretty lively gallops that the brass boys play."

"But they are more suitable for the hunting field than the ballroom. The Post horn gallop could be carnage" said Mrs Walker. As the representative woman on the committee, she felt she had to fight the distaff corner a bit. Cook didn't really count much until it came to the food.

"Should we ask if Michael is free?"

"Who?" asked Cosmo.

"Michael. Of *Michael and All Angels*? The Rock Band. He lives in the village now. They did that splendid thing on the landing craft at the end of the regatta. Don't you remember?"

"I remember that they were terribly loud. This is an old house, Hives, and the Long Gallery- we are using the Long Gallery, I presume? No point in opening up the Ballroom just for a bit of a thrash- I'm not sure of the state of the foundations. We wouldn't want anything too loud."

Mrs Walker tried a separate tack.

"I'm told our postman plays in a band."

"Old Les plays in band?"

"Les retired several years ago, sir. We have a very conscientious if rather odd-looking young man who favours nose rings, among other things, called Alistair," explained Hives. "I am told that his band have quite a... catholic... repertoire."

"Do you think he could play..." And here his lordship trembled slightly, in anticipation... "Honky Tonk Women"?

When word came back that there were 'no worries' involved in their fulfilling this request and that they could manage most things from the Seventies onwards, with the exception of the Michael Jackson song book, Alistair's band, 'Corn-U-Copia' was engaged.

The guests arrived in a variety of vehicles, which excited Philip who was down for the weekend.

But the young ladies were just as varied in their means of transport as they were in themselves and Philip gleefully noted them down in his spotter's book. One even drove her own tractor.

The favoured vehicles among that generation seemed to be the Mini Clubman, white with black trimmings and tinted windows or the all black VW Polo Sport.

"Common as muck" said Philip, even though no-one was listening and he made a note of not bothering with those who drove them.

He was much more excited by a 2CV *fourgonette*, which became a van once the back seat, no more than a bench, was removed, the favoured mode of transport for the peasant and small trades person in rural France. But that evening, instead of a boot full of live geese or crisp, fresh baguettes, several young ladies, their party frocks carelessly stuffed into duffle bags, were crammed into a bright yellow one and, if their screams of laughter as they came up the drive were anything to go by, they had started the festivity early. Philip was particularly pleased when the owner, a stunning chestnut squeezed impossibly into a pair of skin tight jeans, allowed him to park the car for her.

And then the star of the show arrived: a red Audi TT with the top down. A very pretty girl, already dressed in all white for the ball, was sitting in the passenger's seat while the face of the obviously female driver was hidden behind mask-like dark glasses, her hair sheathed in a black silk scarf. She pulled up in front of the main door and displayed an inordinate amount of leg from a frock that matched her car in her dismount. Philip was magnetically drawn to the car and the driver.

"I say, she's an absolute smasher."

"Isn't she just?" agreed the driver although she wasn't looking at the car.

"How old?"

"Well, she admits to twenty-two but actually she's twenty-four." drawled the other.

"I don't believe it! I didn't think they started building them until '94 and the early ones certainly didn't look like this."

"Oh, the car, you mean." And a pair of beautiful violet eyes looked at him over the top of the dark glasses.

"I thought you meant Luce." And again she turned to look after her passenger, who was introducing herself to Cosmo, and obviously referring to the driver.

"Luce?" asked Philip.

"Short for Lucinda."

"And are you her chaperone?"

"No." And here she paused for effect. "I'm Aurora. Her husband."

After the initial, intended shock, she explained. "To be. We're getting married as soon as her father gets out of hospital. He had a bit of a stroke when we told him. He had rather hoped she'd marry that dreadful Trelawny boy but fortunately, she has seen the light. *Moi*."

"So, she's off the list from the start." Philip said, he thought to himself but obviously not loud enough for the other to hear.

"Oh, so it is a cattle-market. Rather what I thought,"

Philip tried a little reconstruction. Having observed a jewel on Lucinda's chest, he said:

"That's a rather jolly broach. Family heirloom?"

"No, I had it made. Lapis lazuli, Beryl and Topaz, all set in gold."

"Does it mean anything?"

"The initials! LGBT!"

"Oh, that, "said Philip. "I had to have someone explain it to me- I thought it was an exceptionally large sandwich."

"Ok, I get the BLT bit- what about the G?"

"Bacon, lettuce, tomato. And gherkin?"

She snorted derisively and loped away, in the direction of Lucinda, whom she met with a full-on kiss, which encouraged Cosmo to move on to his next guest.

There was a distinct air of disappointment among the passengers of the bread van, when they surveyed the other guests who appeared to be almost entirely female, but then the rugby boys arrived. They turned up *'en masse'*, as they knew very well that whenever they got together, things tended to end up rather messily and the club captain, who had accepted the invitation on their behalf, had insisted that they be transported to and from the event in a local coach. That way, he could be sure that none of his boys had disgraced himself or gone off into the bushes with one of the female guests.

"No bonking, leastways not on the premises. You can arrange future action verbally if you get lucky, but Mr Hives insisted that the event was rather like the County Show; the goods were there for inspection, not investigation. You can look but you mustn't touch too much."

So the boys came by bus. And things looked up.

One or two of the trendy career girls from London caused something of a fracas when they asked Cook- who was reigning over the buffet, magnificent in its display of hams, ribs of beef, full poached salmon, quiches, egg and bacon pies and many other local specialities, not least her award-winning pasties- where the vegan options were.

Cook turned to Mrs Walker who was helping serve and said: "Edie, I thought I'd 'eard just about every bit a' bad langwidge, what with Hezekiah bein' my cousin an' all, but that's a word I never thought I'd 'ear, not at Mena Dhu. Tis nigh on unpatriotic!"

Mrs Walker tried to rescue the situation.

"There's parsley on the ham sandwich plate, if that's any good to you. And we do have stuff in the kitchen for the decoration, so we could knock up a salad for you but we'd a' liked a bit of notice. Can you eat strawberries?"

When they admitted that they could and would, Mrs Walker added: "But I suppose clotted cream is out of the question. It does come from downtrodden, exploited cows, you know."

The rugby boys had hoped that they would be something of a hit by all wearing special black and silver bow ties, the colours of Cornwall.

Legend had it that St Piran, the patron saint, had been thrown into Dublin Bay by his parishioners, weighed down by a millstone but *mirabile dictu* had floated all the way to Cornwall. One day, as he went to cook his breakfast, he chose a stone as a hearth upon which he laid his fire. At the end of his meal, he discovered a stream of molten silver metal running from the stone and that, they do say, is how St Piran discovered tin and gave Cornwall its colours- black for the fireplace and silver for the tin. The fact that the Cornish had been mining and exporting tin since before the time of Christ does not appear to daunt the faithful.

However, they were rather upstaged by the hosts: they wore the Cornish tartan, either in the case of Hives and Philip in the bow tie and cummerbund version, or the ladies in a sash, or Sir Cosmo himself, who wore the full regalia, and this was black and gold. It appeared that in their version of the legend, the metal that ran from the stone was gold but that there wasn't very much of it to go around, so it had been changed to the more plentiful tin.

As soon as the haunting, never-to-be-forgotten irregular rhythm on the crazy cowbell was tapped out by the Corn-U-Copia's drummer and the band struck up 'Honky Tonk Women', Cosmo was galvanised.

He grabbed the nearest girl, who happened to be the tractor-driver, Grace, and took to the floor in a remarkable attempt to waltz to the Rolling Stones. The rest took this as a sign and the dancing began.

Things had been going swimmingly when suddenly, Aurora, Lucinda's 'husband' gave out a screech that, devoid of its honeyed Hampstead overtones, betrayed her Camberwell origins.

"Nah! It's a fuckin' pap!" whereupon she threw Lucinda's skirt over the girl's head, hiding those well-known features from prying lenses but revealing more intimate ones, enticingly clad in tight white panties, a suspender belt and white stockings, thereby realising many of the lads' recent fantasies.

"If 'er dad sees us, 'e'd pop 'is clogs, deffo. Get the bastard's camera."

The rugby boys needed no second word. The supposed 'paparazzo' had been shooting through a window and was high tailing it down the drive but had not taken into consideration the nature of most of the males and he was no match for fit young rugby players, one of whom, a wing three-quarter- had had a trial for Cornish Pirates; he had hurdled the window sill, raced after the intruder and tackled him before he was half-way, whereupon the rest- the forwards- practised their rucking technique and shoe-ed the intruder around the gravel drive. Then Nathan, the seventeen stone second row who worked with Jago and H. as a labourer, who had honed his physique by humping breeze-blocks and had portrayed *Thisb*e in their Mechanicals play, picked up the interloper by jacket lapels and recognised him.

"Hey, it's that plonker what Jago give the gurnard blow-job to!"

Indeed, Cyril Oliphant it was! And Jago had indeed inserted a non-too fresh gurnard down the front of Cyril's trousers in payment for an earlier indiscretion.

While Cyril spluttered, the scrum half, naturally quick witted, extracted the photo card from the camera and pocketed it.

"But I'm Press!"

"Bollocks" replied Nathan.

"Let's see your accreditation" said the scrum half.

"Well... you don't need it these days."

"Bollocks" repeated Nathan.

Hives had caught up with the melee by now.

"Excuse me, sir but this is a private party."

"But the people have a right to know!"

"Which people? And know what?"

"Well... the people. And know what is going on."

Nathan remembered.

"They caught 'en 'anging around they meetin's they 'ad up the old admiral's place. Ask me, 'e's just a nosey bloody Parker. Fuckin' peepin' Tom." Nathan had picked up much of his fluency from Hezekiah.

"If you will leave, we shall take it no further. If not, his Lordship will and does prosecute for trespass."

"Where's my camera? If you've damaged my camera, it'll be me who'll be doing the prosecuting."

"This what you're referring to?" asked the scrum half as he handed back the camera.

"Yes well..."

"These young men," said Hives, "have something of a reputation for de-bagging. Removing unpopular people of their trouser-wear. I trust you are not going to continue and force them to give a demonstration?"

Cyril could not think of anything to say and so left quickly. It was not until he got back to his cottage that he realised that there was no card in the camera.

Cyril Oliphant was arguably the least popular person in the village. He imagined himself to be some sort of chronicler of the life of Cornwall, possibly a Causley or a Rowse, even another Quiller Couch; he claimed to be a published poet which, in the strictest sense, was true. The editor of the local parish magazine, forever starved of material, had once agreed to print a verse of his called 'My Favourite Things' which began:

"I love the smell of burning clutch

And bonnets far too hot to touch."

But rather than sit and write, he tended to simply sit, possibly take notes and positively snoop. He was still bearing the scars of a blow on his bulbous nose from the local inspector of police following a failed drugs raid on the night of the Regatta. He fancied himself as a man of the sea, even if he never actually went on it and so took to dressing like one: the shabby Harlequin-style quartered rugby shirt- the originals were worn by the men off the Falmouth oyster boats but now the chains of up-market yachties' outfitters that had sprung up all along the south coat were marketing them at exorbitant prices- the faded pink trousers much favoured by the elder members of the sailing clubs, topped off by whichever of his jaunty caps he thought suited him that day- today a Che Guevara- which hid his grey thinning locks which rather resembled used Brillo pads. Sadly, whatever effect he was after was completely spoiled by the grey woollen ankle-socks with just a hint of doughy flesh visible above the open-toed sandals. He had recently begun to sport a sort of goatee beard which he felt made him look both arty and trendy at the same time but really, any self-respecting rat would have been ashamed to have had that following it around.

He liked it to be known that he lived off his royalties but in fact his old mother in Tonbridge Wells gave him a monthly allowance out of the very healthy pension that her late husband, his erstwhile father, had left her; and she was happy to do so in order to keep him out of her expensively blued hair, and her world of bridge, gin and Spanish gardeners. Cyril could afford to hire one of the cottages without a sea view at a reasonable annual rent and he had modest tastes. Had the allowance been greater, the tastes would have been less modest. He had ambitions, almost all entirely unfulfilled.

Back at the Ball, things were beginning to wind down. It was that time in the evening when guests, in pairs would either wander off upstairs, if the party was indoors, or off into the woods were it 'al fresco'. Such events having been specifically proscribed from the start, they all knew it wasn't going to happen. Leastways, not at Mena Dhu, but they were, for the most part, healthy young people in the primes of their lives and further entertainment was inevitable. Trysts and assignations had been arranged over the pasties and the pies and while the men were returned dutifully to the rugby club, the coach was followed by a procession of smoked-windowed Mini Coopers, CV fourgonettes and one tractor.

As Cosmo and Philip were joined by Hives and Mrs Walker in the small drawing room over a tray of Ovaltine and a decanter of port- Cook having retired already, still chuntering on about the vegans- the consensus was that a good time had been had by almost all, but that his Lordship was nowhere nearer his goal that he had been before.

Chapter Eight

While the pub was a safe house and sanctuary for the men of the village and had been since time immemorial, as long as they had the price of a pint, the women too had their haunt, now that cheap white goods had taken most of the time-consuming drudgery and sweat out of the daily grind of washing, mending and cooking. While it was still 'only a hussy' that would go to the pub on her own- "An' there's a fair few of they, too, an' all, downalong"- most of the older generation of womankind felt both their reputations safe and their femininity intact if they went to the 'caff' on their own.

The only thing brazen about the establishment was the sign hanging outside *'The Copper Kettle'* on the quay and that was hand-painted. Inside was the type of tea room seen throughout the country; half-length, pink check gingham curtains coyly maintaining a certain mystique, so that anyone interested had to apply nose to pane to discover what was going on inside. What made it particular, though, was the fact that almost everything they sold- apart from the beans- had been baked in those small rooms, so the very smell brought in the customers.

And almost every day, certainly during clement weather, there would be, after ten a.m., a core coterie of ladies, all over fifty and most of whom would not see seventy again, putting the world in general and the village in particular to rights and then, after eleven, another 'naicer' group, none of whom was indigenous but they were certainly long-standing, would take over.

The instigator of this excellence was Bunty Williams, a comparative newcomer to living in Porthwallow but one of those rare erstwhile second-home owners who had actually fulfilled the promise of "we'll be here to live full-time once Brian actually retires."

A mild heart attack had forced Brian to take his doctor's advice: "twenty more years if you stop today, old man, or you'll be dead in one if you don't". So they had sold up in Gloucestershire and spent a lot of money doing up what had been the holiday home. Hezekiah had had a heyday. Brian did take the advice and so filled his time with walking the dog and building a model railway in the garden- something he had promised himself and Bunty since his wedding day, that he would do when he had both room and time. Now he had both and no excuse. But Bunty was a do-er.

Raising three golden children who had, between them, produced seven grandchildren had been a doddle. It was what one had been bred for, after all, what?! So she had looked around for something to do now that they were off her hands and far enough away to discourage regular visits.

She had opened her first garden centre just at the right time, 1996, so that when 'Ground Force' hit the television screens and gardening became more popular than cooking or sex among the readers of the 'Daily Mail', she was in a position to expand and capitalise, although she, at least, did retain her foundation garments. By the time she sold up, at the top of the market, she had had a chain and hence had, in her own right, a lot of money.

Breezing into Porthwallow, she took one look at the harbour and having realised what was missing, namely a tea-room, rectified it.

"Tis lovely," was the general opinion.

The majority of her regulars were women of a certain age and older. Most had lived in Porthwallow all their lives and had some wonderful stories about a time when things were simpler but the basics were very similar; those in the other group had retired to the village and so added depth, breadth and colour to the conversation, which was incessant.

At the core of the first coven was usually Betty; she had an unpronounceable and certainly un-spellable surname because she had been married- albeit briefly- to a Pole. At the end of the war, there had been thousands of Poles at something of a loose end in Britain and an equal number of young ladies ready to show their gratitude for having been liberated. Betty, although only fifteen at the end of the war had been particularly willing to acknowledge her debt. Amidst the partakers of this generosity had been the appropriately named Bonawentura J drzejewicz and when it became known that a little Slav seed had taken root in Cornish soil, he did the honourable thing and married her. Fortunately for all, he was recalled to help rebuild his homeland, where he died, and while Betty did have other children, she maintained the exotic name of her first love.

Betty was getting on and had a tendency to doze, so the unofficial chair of this unofficial women's union was taken by Mrs Janice Tomlinson. A good fifteen years younger that Betty, she had had ambitions and so had got a job in a shop in St Austell. This meant that her circle of beaux had not been limited to Porthwallow and she had married a man from Mevagissey. Her father had been a fisherman and she had vowed that a fisherman was the last thing her husband would be. Sadly, it was, for he had drowned some forty years ago.

Whenever such a tragedy hits one of these small communities, all the petty, mundane niggles tend to be forgotten in a surge of generosity. Cash, furniture, clothing, even foodstuffs, along with well-intentioned if ill-spelled cards would appear at the door of the Methodist chapel, even though the minister had had to leave years ago and the place was usually locked in order to keep atheistic fornicators, in search of somewhere dry, at bay. However, on these occasions an unspoken law prevailed and nothing was touched, although for some it was chance to shift some old clothes and for others to pass on that hideous pink plaster vase that appeared and did the rounds at every white elephant stall at every bring-and-buy coffee morning.

They had been used to large families in small cottages, so Janice easily found space back with her mother while a couple of children were easily lost in the scrum that ran harmless riot through the place. The children were now in their late forties and both had married and moved up to Clay Country, the villages above St Austell that had flourished with the china clay and declined with it as well.

These stalwarts were joined by Ida Templeton who had travelled. Everybody knew this as soon as she opened her mouth. Her vowels were pure 'East Enders'. She had come to Looe back in the Seventies to work for the summer; there was always a need for waitresses or barmaids, especially if they came from London with the clothes and dance moves of the day. She was very popular on the dance floor of *The Boscarne Hotel* of a Saturday night and, if some local lad was lucky, on the beach beside it after. Pregnant by the end of the summer, there was nowhere back in Battersea for her and fortunately, her luck was in with the man she met. It was very rare for Bert Hunkin to come over from Porthwallow, out with the lads, and rightly, couldn't believe his luck when that night ended as it had. It was not until Ida came knocking on his mother's door in Porthwallow that he discovered the truth in the physics teacher's words that every action had an equal and opposite reaction.

But really, Ida was exactly what Bert had wanted, a bit of life, while Bert offered Ida all the security that she had never had in London. Bert was working on the docks over in Fowey, again resurgent prior to the next decline in china clay prices; he had his own little cottage in the village and they had been very happy. And still were.

Then there was Maggie Tregenza, who probably knew more about more people in the village than anyone, as she had been the dispenser at the village surgery for more than thirty years. Her husband, Colin, had run a garage and petrol station in the village until age and the competition from the monstrous supermarkets had forced him to close. He still tinkered with the cars of old friends in the village and kept them in far better nick than the commercial boys in town.

He also followed the horses. Not with bucket and shovel for the roses but the racing, the steeplechasing in particular and the fortnights that included the Cheltenham Festival and finished with the Grand National were the high spots of his year. He would bet within reason- in fact, before the legalization of betting, he had been the local runner for a bookie in St Austell, something which took him out of the village and gave him something of a social life. The advent of the telephone and the opening of the high street shops made everything so much easier and legal, but a certain frisson had gone out of his life. He did not understand computers and so had not discovered the on-line business, which was probably just as well, as his walk down to the corner shop for the Racing Post each morning was now just about all the exercise that he got. Maggie was deemed the fount of all knowledge rather than opinionated fancy, which was Betty's speciality.

"Young Cosmo's gettin' wed."

"'Oo says?!"

"Had it from young Monica who works up the Big 'Ouse. Reckon you'm in with a chance then, maid?"

This was addressed by Janice to Jenny whose shocked reaction it had been. Acting as catalyst and motive force in these gatherings, Jenny Thomas was employed by Bunty as waitress, commis chef and general mover and shaker. It was just one of a few little jobs that she had to keep her busy: she was by now the motivating force behind the theatre club, had worked tirelessly during the Festival to raise money for the new Village Hall and had had a brief but heady whirl with the one-legged rigger who had come down from London to lend his lighting expertise to the event.

If not exactly renowned for such behaviour, there was a regular string of such encounters in her past. Born in the village in the late 1960s, she had followed a number of her friends to the local sixth-form college- "it'll be a good laugh"- and thoroughly misbehaved in all of the classes that she turned up for, with the notable exception of hair-dressing, mainly because it was 'hand's on' and there wasn't a back row in which she could slump and insult the teachers, which had been her primary pursuit in other subjects. She came out with a qualification in hair-dressing and beauty and looked around, waiting for Life to begin and while she waited, practised both on her friends and herself, with the more outrageous hair-dos that the big stars in the magazines wore, so that when they hit the dance floor of *The Boscarne*, in near-by Looe of a Friday, it looked like every night was Walpurgisnacht. Their more remarkable *bouffants* set her imagination racing. Opposite a washed and wiped face in the mirror, she began to fantasize about who that face might be or might become on the inside as well as the outside; then a chance encounter in the Ladies at *The Boscarne* led to an introduction to a local am-dram group, after which there was no looking back. She had found her element. True, she would often still end Friday nights on her back in one of the beach huts with blokes whose liberal use of Brut could not disguise the fact that they had been fishing all week, but she had found something to fill her days and more and more of her nights.

In the village, a remarkable set of coincidences had meant that there were several couples, incomers mainly, who had a passion for Amateur Dramatics. And after an unexpectedly successful '*Good Old Days*' when party pieces were aired in the Church Hall, the Porthwallow Players had been born.

Into this magic circle, Jenny had entered. As a still young juvenile lead, she was a God-send and played opposite a number of the husbands. The fact that she also played about with a number of the husbands was, for the most part, ignored. After all, it had been the Eighties, the summer of Love, long gone but not forgotten; and some of those earlier parties had often ended with the car-keys in a bowl on the coffee table when it was simply a matter of trying to avoid the owner of the bicycle clips.

Sadly, most of the couples had been of a similar age, which

meant that they had all died at a similar age and with that spate of funerals out at the Wallow, went the Theatre Club.

Jenny had been married briefly to one of those beach encounters, but he was off the Scottish boats and as the fish diminished down south, so did the amount of time he stayed in these waters. Last she had heard of him, he was living in Buckie and working off-shore on the oil rigs. But a bi-product of their transient marriage had been Jim, a fine lad, nearly thirty now, who had joined the Navy as soon as he had been able. The Admiral had lent a hand here; he had had his eye on the boy ever since there had been a slight chance that the child might be the fruit of a visit by one of the Admiral's sons, a hedge-fund manager from New York whose vacation had coincided with the fishing fleet being at sea. His expensive champagne had had the desired effect upon Jenny and he marked it down as both much cheaper and more enjoyable that any escort on Fifth Avenue. A discreet DNA test after the boy was born had proved the Hawkins' fears to be ungrounded but presents would arrive irregularly via the Admiral for Jenny. She prided herself on having brought the child up alone, albeit in the tight community of Porthwallow where every other man was his 'uncle' and every woman his 'auntie', some even related by blood. Her current partner was a long-distance lorry driver which made things comparatively straight-forward. She still went dancing at *The Boscarne* now and then but now never again ended the night on the beach.

Discovering herself to be pregnant, she had married one

of the fishermen but he had gone back to Buckie with his boat. Currently she lived with the long-distance lorry driver who preferred his own company in his cab with his extensive collection of special DVDs bought abroad, to life in a little Cornish village, which meant that she had time for 'one of her moments' more often these days in Newquay. And one of those moments had involved the young Sir Cosmo de Coverlet. At least, so she believed.

In answer to Janice's question, she said a definite 'No'.

"He may enjoy his occasional nights out- I know some girls in Newquay who... 'know' him. Very generous, he is." And then added hastily: "Or so I'm told. But when it comes to marriage... no, it'll be some posh totty from upalong."

Chapter Nine

"Have you actually met Sir Cosmo?" asked Michael.

This was at the next selection committee meeting, after he had accepted happily, as had the Vicar and Jeremy. Michael was taking advantage of his gradual acceptance in the village to discover more about the local history. People no longer stopped talking to gaze at him as he entered the pub, he was no longer 'matey, that rock star up the Garden 'Ouse so much as 'Michael'. H. had once made the mistake of calling him 'Mick', either out of misplaced congeniality or rock-star confusion, but only the once.

"It's Michael, Hezekiah, Michael. Not Mick, nor Mike but Michael. You can muddle up the arch angels if you must, but don't forget- Michael."

It was the few times like these that you could recognise the iron in the velvet glove that had been necessary for Michael to get to where he had been.

Michael Donohue had moved, with his young son, Jake, into Porthwallow after the death of his wife. At first, it had seemed, to outsiders, that they were seeking a hermitage, a refuge, but gradually, the village in general, and Sandy, a young teacher in particular had brought him out of himself and he had headlined the last Regatta with his world-renowned band, *Michael and the Angels.* That had been part of the scheme to raise money to rebuild the Village Hall, destroyed in the winter floods and once a top-line rock band, more used to arenas than quaysides, sailed in on a landing craft, everyone knew who he was.

It was true that they had had to resort to a modern version of the ancient practise of smuggling to achieve their goal, but he had been deeply involved in that as well.

The Vicar and his partner, Jeremy, and Michael, who had taken delightedly to the idea of playing for the village- another sign of being accepted for who, rather than what he was, had joined the selection committee. H. was a builder with the filthiest mouth known to man, but things were improving. His contribution to the festival had been to play Starveling, the lantern in the Mechanicals play and from being one of the most self-centred beings in the village, he had begun to understand collaboration- team work. Similarly, the Vicar was finding himself and Jeremy his partner for well over twenty years, before a sympathetic bishop had moved them from inner city purgatory to coastal paradise- more accepted in a real way. Folk had always called out: 'Morning, Vicar', but since his performance as Peter Quince, they were realising that there was a real person inside that dog-collar. Jeremy helped with everything that was not ostentatious while Jago did what he could. In the summer, he went fishing, in the winter a jobbing builder, he worked with H. He had seen the world, walked round virtually all of it, but had found that nowhere beat Porthwallow, with all its failings and so had come home. He was holding forth at one table, the rest of the bar being seemingly empty

"Oh yes," said Jago. "His old father, now, 'e 'adn't been seen for a good long while. They do say tis only machines as keep 'im goin' but the young lord..."

"'Lord'?" Michael put down his bottle of Peroni in surprise. (It was a measure of the extent in which Michael had been accepted that not only had Charlie Onions, the landlord, ordered crates of the beer especially for him but others had started to drink it as well.)

"Ais." said Jago. "They'm real aristocracy" said Jago.

"Real old aristocracy" added H.

"I do say 'young', but 'e must be fifty if 'e's a day."

Michael gestured to Tegan who was behind the bar and called: "Same again, please- and can I put it on my tab, please, Charlie?"

Charlie was not always prepared to run tabs, especially for visitors whom he did not know, but considering the fact that everyone knew Michael and most where he lived and that there was little doubting that he could afford it- their latest album 'One and All' had been at the top of the charts for a month and they had already sold millions- so the old man nodded.

"Trevor?" He asked the vicar first, an inherent bi-product of a Cathedral school education.

"Something soft. I still have Evensong. An orange juice, please."

Jago cocked an eye at Jeremy who looked at the table when

replying: "Ginger beer, please." H. couldn't help himself but changed his snigger to a cough and said: "Proper job", echoed by Nathan while Jago said: "Guinness, please, maid. In a clean glass!"

"And another of these, please? Thanks", "said Michael, waving the beer bottle towards her," Now. Tell us about it."

The band of six drew a little closer, like a company of conspirators.

"How are you on local 'istory?" asked Jago, inhaling the top off his pint of Guinness.

"When you say 'local'- I know something about the Civil War down here. Somebody nearly shot King Charles near Fowey. And there's all the stories about pirates. And smuggling." This brought a chuckle all round as they all been in on their recent excursion into 'the Trade.'

"Naw!"said Jago, relishing his position as focus of attention. "We'm goin' way back. Before the Normans!"

"The Romans?!"

"See?" Jago leaned back and gestured expansively to the room.

"Tis a terrible indictment on our teachin' of 'ist'ry if an intelligent man like you can't think of nothin' beween the Normans and the Romans-"

Michael defended himself.

"Well, they do call it the Dark Ages-"

"Tis true", agreed H. who felt he was backing a winner in

siding with Michael.

"And I always tended to have music lessons during History." said Michael.

"Excuses!"

"Alfred and the Cakes." This came from H. who objected to being thought of as ignorant.

"Suppose that's something. What about all that tosh over Tintagel? Merlin and that?!" asked Jago.

"Oh, you mean King Arthur?"

Tegan butted in.

"Most of Britain claims King Arthur. Right up to Cumbria. Not to mention the Welsh."

"So we won't." said Jago. "Bit of a myth, some do say, really, but all they minor kings- so called knights- they existed. May not have all sat round a round table in suits as'd take a can opener to get in and out of but they existed. Us had ours n' all, called King Mark-"

"Ah, the husband of Isolde- Uncle of Tristan-" said Michael, glad not to appear too ignorant.

"That's not bad-but you'm a musician- 'e's in that dreadful opera."

"Yes," said Michael, "I have to agree that Wagner is an acquired taste-"

"But seeing' as 'ow we inn't gonna acquire it-" huffed H. "Can you 'lucidate? Or at least get on?"

"Now, backalong, kings weren't what we'd call kings- Buck 'ouse, all crowns an' the Christmas Speech 'an all that- twas a matter of translation too. They was what they called '*duc*s.'"

"'Ducks'? What? Like Aylsbury?"

"Naw- Pillock. '*Duc*' is your actual Latin-"

"Leader," said Michael, dredging through memories of time spent in the shadows of the cathedral at which he had been a choral scholar.

"Very impressive! So the leader of the tribe or the band whatever, 'e was the Duc, and Duc in't far away from Duke and this Mark, 'e was a 'ard old sod, seems, an' 'e was the leader or Duke of the Cornish. Years later, some English king give 'is babby the name o' "Duke o' Cornwall"- and that's what they d'call old Charlie boy now but don't mean nothin', not to Sir Cosmo and 'is family. Cos they'm the real royal family-leastways of Cornwall- don't give toss about upcountry."

"Edward the Third."

It was Michael who supplied the company with the specifics, but it was of no great import in the run of things.

"See", said Jago," Now- where are we?"

"Eh?" asked H.

"Where?"

"Porthwallow, you twat-"

"H.!"

Tegan had formed an alliance with the vicar to improve Hezekiah's language.

"No- more specific?"

"You mean the pub?" asked Michael.

"Ais! *The Cover*- or more specifically, *The de Coverlet Arms*."

He swallowed half a pint of Guinness. "Now, do you know the old sayin', 'Wrong side o' the blanket?'"

"Yes, well-" Michael was being modest, not wishing to dominate the quiz.

But H. helped out.

"Bastard!"

"H!" said Tegan sharply.

"No-that's it, in't it, Vicar?" he checked with Trevor, who bowed but it was Jago who continued.

"Ais. An' what's another word fer a blanket? 'Coverlet'. Tis an ancient name, before the Normans even- De Coverlet, 'from the wrong side of the blanket' or 'the bastard'. They was all at it- even William the Conqueror, 'e was William the Bastard. Sir Cosmo's great, great dunno how many times 'great' grandfather, they said, was a bastard. A 'De Coverlet', from the blanket. Now, just think if they'd've allowed bastards to become king! All those kings producing dozens of illegitimate kids but couldn't manage a legit one with the wife!"

"I knows one or two round 'ere like that!" said H and laughed out loud.

"And d'you know whose bastard 'e was?" Jago knew how to tell a story, having strung dozens of emmets along with his tales. But this story he had never told, until now.

"Followin' the laws they 'ad backalong about 'bastards'? Only Tristan and Yseut's! Which could a made matey the rightful king of Cornwall. All England, possibly. Yes!! If our lot up the Big 'Ouse had ever had any get-up-and-go, pulled its finger out and wasn't quite so..."

"Individual?" suggested Jeremy.

"Thanks- I mean, there's one o' them, 'is cousin, Philip, thinks 'e's a car! No, if they wasn't a couple of diamonds short of a tiara, the world'd be a different place. But you've 'eard the term 'dreckly'?"

Michael nodded, still learning not to expect local workmen at a time when they swear blind they'll be there.

"They do epitomise the meaning of 'dreckly'- somewhat more later than *'manana'*. But there'd 've been none of your nastiness if 'n we'd have let bastards on to the throne. Henry I had twenty or more to choose the best from, Henry VIII could have made done with just the one wife- two at a push. Charles II- 'e 'ad dozens of the little bastards to choose from but didn't."

"But what about they over at Mena Dhu?" H. was getting interested.

"Like I said, us 'as got to go back to that there legend about Tristan and Isolde. Detail dun't matter for the why and wherefore but basically, Tristan was knockin' off this maid he'd fetched back from Ireland who was supposed to be (a) goin' to be 'is uncle's missus and (b) a virgin, and they was caught, see, at it, just about, but rather than be 'anged..." Jago's flow was interrupted.

"An' castrated, they do say." said H. whose knowledge of history was founded on such nuggets of detail.

"Yes, thank you, H.- unlikely, given the rest of the story.

Where was I? Rather than' anged, 'e burst out through the window of the 'ermit's cell where he had taken sanctuary on the cliff top and leaped down the cliff, jumped into the sea and swam away-"

"And that's why they call that cliff, in front of the Big House, "Tristan' Leap' ?!" This time it was Tegan who was adding a piece of local knowledge.

"Yeas! And that 'ermit's cell was the foundations of Mena Dhu!"

"Yes, but, what about our Lord Cosmo?" asked Michael. "Nowadays seems a long way from the Dark Ages?"

"Well, they'm right in callin' them the Dark Ages," said Jago, in rather an embarrassed way, "Cos things get very dark 'ereabouts and no-one really knows but- they do say, on that boat over, they was at it- you know, nookie- and rather than feel sinful, they got the skipper to marry them! Yes. And as you know, married by a captain on board ship is same as in holy church. In't that right, Vicar?"

"Well..." Trevor did not want to bring up the actual legal truth, so prevaricated. "Well …"

"Anyway," Jago did not want to break the flow." Yseut 'ad a babby- Tristan's babby- Tristan's lawful babby- an' 'e"... And here he drew them all closer-

"Was the first."

"First what?" asked H.

"De Coverlet. An' young Sir Cosmo is the latest. In direct line of descent. And they do say, 'e 'as every right to be the real

King of Cornwall, and probably of England too!"

Five of the listeners drew in their breath.

"Bugger me!" said H., forgetting himself. "Sorry, Vicar."

"I think, just this once, you are to be forgiven."

In the next stall, Cyril Oliphant, who had been dividing his time between trying to eavesdrop the history lesson and ogle Tegan's magnificent bust, nearly choked on his cheese and onion crisps, washed down with sparkling mineral water. Spluttering and leaving an unpleasant spray of soggy potato shards in the air behind him, he bolted for the door. The others were each so lost in his own thoughts that no-one noticed.

Chapter Ten

After the gurnard incident which had set him against the village and the threat of debagging after the ball, Cyril Oliphant now had a cause: revenge. He was also one of the few people living in the village who not only had a computer but also knew how to use it.

He was seated in front of the computer screen, Googling. There was so much about the various versions of the Tristan legend, but it was just as likely that the garbled version that he had just overheard from Jago was as true as any of the other, reflecting more the position of the authors than the veracity of their tale.

"The true King of Cornwall? Of England, even!"

Cyril's head spun; true, it did not take a great deal to do this but it was incredible. And if it were true? Who would buy it? Literally?

Cyril had already had one nasty experience with contacting the press, even though his story had been true.

He had managed to discover- all right, eavesdrop- the meeting at which Michael Donohoe had agreed to come out of self-imposed retirement and play, with his band, the Angels, at the Regatta. However, none of the nationals were interested in any story from further afield than Staines, unless it was

Love Island, and the local papers were dubious, apart from the ambitious young editor of the Mid Cornwall Gazette, who had printed the story and had his laptop destroyed by some sinister strangers for his pains. They had also visited Cyril and had left him in no uncertain doubt that such behaviour should not occur again.

The BBC TV did not reply to input from locals, keeping their airways free for stories about rail strikes and seal pups. The ITV were terminally uncertain of their identity and local radio needed advertising revenue, not originality.

So the media were non-starters. Who would be interested in the true king? A book? But it would be so much work, researching and then actually writing the thing. He would need a production company to do that. The fact that the real British Royal family was currently residing in an ancient country house on a clifftop in Cornwall- who would care enough to make it worth his while?

The current Royal family, most likely. So, how to get through to them? Of course, Google!

He tried 'Contact the Royal family' but the headings included writing directly to Her Majesty and somehow, even someone as insensitive as Cyril realised that she would not welcome a letter from a member of the public putting an end to her historic reign just like that; there was an address for the Public Information Office, which again he felt unsuitable while the Press Offices did not bear contemplation.

If not the Press not the Royal Family, how about the

Government? The Conservatives would conveniently mislay the story, as they had so much to lose; the Labour party could not be trusted to handle it while the Liberals, even with their history of past Cornish glories, would only watch from the side-lines, no matter what was happening. If not the mainline parties, how about something a bit more dangerous, a bit more 'far out'? Or should that be 'a bit further out? Cornish Liberationists? He would have to think on it. But the opportunity of the Fete which was to be held at Mena Dhu was too good to miss.

It was while driving back from his weekly shop at Waitrose in Truro- he had already transferred his purchases into some ASDA bags as he would not have been seen dead carrying Waitrose bags in the village, giving the impressions that (a) he couldn't get what he wanted in the village shop and (b) his were not the tastes of the common people but at least he did not have his luxuries delivered!- that he saw some grafitti daubed onto a wall outside St Austell. It was not of the artistic sort that appears of motorway bridges and seemingly inaccessible walls beside railway lines but it was legible. It read: "Free Cornwall!" Unfortunately, someone with a nice hand and an antique line in humour had added: "With every five gallons." but this exhortation was actually signed, something that appeared to be: 'Breder Kernow'. This was a group he had never heard of and Cyril returned to his faithful Google to know more.

Nothing appeared on Google when prompted by 'Breder Kernow' except for a load of puff about an obscure and recently dead German artist, but Cyril Oliphant did not give up very easily. In his favourite persona of a writer incognito, hinting at, but never actually claiming success, he haunted the local Library, when open. It was warm, it was free and had very pleasant lady assistants about whom he could fantasize. During his next visit, he asked if they knew of 'Breder Kernow', to be told what he knew, that 'Mabyon Kernow' was 'Sons of Cornwall', the local nationalist party and with the aid of the Cornish-English dictionary, they agreed that 'Breder Kernow' must mean 'Brothers of Cornwall'.

"I've seen that somewhere," said one of the ladies.

"Yes," said Cyril, "On a wall outside St Austell."

"No, no" said the lady. "I saw a poster, up near where I live. Up near Lanlivery, on the moor. You could ask at the pub."

Cyril drove his Skoda Favorit into the pretty little hamlet of Lanlivery and asked at the pub for directions.

"Where to?" came the sensible question from behind the bar.

That was when Cyril had to admit that he didn't know and was hoping that they might know something about 'Breder Kernow'.

The young barmaid was about to apologise for her ignorance when an elder gentleman in Vyella and cavalry twill interrupted: "I think you might find that that's what those... dippy hippy types call themselves. Got one of those back-to-nature places out on the moor. Crawl back under a stone, more like, if you ask me. Difficult to find but you take the lane signposted Redmoor. If you reach Redmoor, you'll've gone too far."

Bodmin Moor has none of the beauties of either Exmoor not Dartmoor; no colourful legends, akin to Lorna Doone or *The Hound of the Baskervilles*', with the possible exception of *Jamaica Inn*'. It is a mass of scrub and stone with none of the splendour of the Valley of the Rocks nor the Ten Tors, loured over by the grim, granite prison at Princetown. The best Bodmin had to offer was Brown Willie.

But it was very easy to get lost in its crabby little lanes bordered by stone banks too high to see over. Every now and then there were would be a farm and a cluster of outhouses, often hidden behind high wooden gates, and barbed wire atop the boulders that designated the perimeter of these homesteads and how willing the residents were to welcome visitors. The front yards, once scratched by generations of assorted poultry, were now filled with cars that could have been scrap or might just have been able to have been made roadworthy. And this was the trade of those who lived there. Neither car door would necessarily be of the same colour, similarly the boot and the bonnet, but such niceties did not matter as long as the finished hybrid ran. In days gone by, folk might have called them 'tinkers'; now they just tinkered.

Cyril was totally lost when he saw the very words he was looking for: 'Breder Kernow', painted in the same colour and by the same hand that had advertised their existence on the wall outside St Austell. Beneath it was the word 'Avodya!', and in brackets beneath: (Keep out!) for those few passing travellers who did not have the Cornish.

Cyril stopped the Favorit and got out. From outside, Cyril could hear a hearty row within, most definitely in English, unless the Cornish had adopted the entire English lexicon of swearwords, lock, stock and barrel. When he knocked, there was a sudden silence, then:

"*Pandra venja whei?* "followed very quickly by a whispered; "No, that's not right." "Fuck off!"

"Um," said Cyril, raising his voice, "I'm afraid I don't speak much Cornish. Can we converse in English?"

A small gap appeared in the gates and part of a face became apparent. "What about?" The accent was certainly not Cornish. Cyril rightly assumed that it was male, obviously human but the bits of what else he could see were confusing. It had a long, wispy beard, a mixture of ginger and grey tied in a knot with an upper lip tinted in nicotine brown: the excess of hair over the bottom half of his head was countered by the comparative absence above. While some luggards would sport several days' growth of beard, here there was several days' growth of hair across a previously shaved head. The owner obviously partook enthusiastically of the more disfiguring of personal improvements as there were tattoos across much of his face and where there were not, there were piercings, including one through his tongue which did not aid diction. When he stepped back to allow Cyril to enter, it could be seen that his choice of clothing was as eclectic as his facial adornments. The armless, knee-length coat, by the smell of it, probably originated from the region of the Khyber Pass, most likely via Carnaby Street in the early Seventies. He had a faded purple granddad collarless shirt beneath the coat and wore lime-green trousers that he liked to describe as 'hareem pants' but most would call 'jogging bottoms'. Multi-coloured leather boots bottomed off this ensemble.

"Hi- I'm Auroch. And this is Gaia."

Cyril was still absorbing the vision that was Auroch and so was hardly ready for the next revelation. 'Gaia' was rightly named after the ancient Earth Goddess as she definitely resembled those early clay statuettes, all bust and belly. She had long, waist length hair which she wore unadorned, unrestrained and unwashed and sported a rainbow-coloured kaftan over a floaty skirt, not very white long-johns and almost obligatory Doc Marten boots. She shared the taste for tattoos and piercings with Auroch which meant that, sadly, both of them appeared to have a very nasty skin infection which only on closer examination proved to be Art.

"Wot you looking at?" she asked, aggressively.

"Well" said Cyril, "I was looking for the 'Breder Kernow'."

"Why?"

"Well, I might have a business proposition."

"Wot jew mean- 'proposition'?" asked Auroch. "Jew mean, like, 'monay'?"

Mena Dhu

In the counting house at Mena Dhu, in a rarely disturbed corner, there was an oaken strongbox, what had come to be known as the Endowment Coffer, the key to which had, by some of Cosmo's ancestors, been worn round their necks and at no time, not even at the height of engendering, been known to leave their necks . Given Cosmo's lackadaisical approach to everything, including copulation, the key now hung on the back of the door but it opened the lock to the box within which, along with all the deeds to the local properties that the family owned, lay some of the most valuable and possibly explosive documents in the world: the agreements between the many generations of the de Coverlet family, renewed by the so-called regents of the time, to allow the family to exist serene and untroubled, so long as they did not claim what was, arguably, rightly theirs, namely not only the country known as the kingdom of Cornwall but also the lands belonging to the Lord of the Cliffs, the Master of the Strands, Prince of Armorica and Seigneur of le Bas Pays, more commonly known as Lyonesse.

Considering that the last two had been under the sea for more than two thousand years, obviously these documents were as old as they were valuable. On the rare occasions that they had been contested, just one look at the actual writings had silenced any opposition, while a brief totting of their potential investment value had been unanswerable. The representatives simply countersigned the warrants and agreed to whatever the de Coverlets had asked. Fortunately, there was not, nor had there ever been, an aspirational bone in their bodies nor gene in their make-up so the governments of the day had at least one fewer potential headache.

However, there was in every government since Simon de Monfort, a 'de Coverlet plenipotentiary'; prior to that, the job had been part of the Bishop of Exeter's.

The current civil servant, newly appointed to this role, was a certain Mark Tregaskis. First at Oxford in P.P.E., he had been reading into the background of his new job and the more he read, the more astounded he became. And the more astounded he became, the more abstrusely his brain began to function. It might be fun to destroy some outdated Cornish clan, he thought, outrageously rich and totally unproductive.

As the name suggested, he was a Cornish boy. Some mighty mandarin high in the labyrinth that is the British Civil Service thought that it would be screamingly funny for a boy from the Duchy to handle this most byzantine of local matters and so he it was who had access to the matters.

No-one would recognise the fat bespectacled swot, all parka and Doc Martens, who had won a place at the local independent school where he discovered that not only was it useful being clever but that there was a sexual thrill in manipulating. Mark was no yokel from a picturesque fishing village but a hard boy, son of tin miners out West who had had the life-style of generations destroyed by greedy businessmen and weak politicians.

Mena Dhu

He was neither one of the village thugs who had delighted in kicking the shit out of him in the rugby lessons, overseen by a former county player who also despised fat boys nor, when he got to his new school, of obvious prefect material, like the sons of the middle-class incomers who ruled the roost. However, he had caught the exercise bug at Oxford and was amazed at the change in his life brought about by the loss of four stone and the acquisition of a pair of contact lenses.

Nearly good-looking, he was now sought by pretty Freshers from St Hilda's for help with their Economics essays, in exchange for infra mural activities.

Nowadays the man who answered to that name was the epitome of metropolitan cool, from his discretely tinted hair via his Brunico charcoal coloured suit, his blue shirt and yellow silk tie to his Crockett and Jones shoes, with the spectacularly garish socks only occasionally visible. They were very evident at the moment as he sat back in the leather wing armchair in front of a fire at The Carlton.

"I want you to keep this under your hat, Cat; it's quite incredible."

His current interlocutor was another immaculately turned-out civil servant, Catriona Douglas, fully intent on bursting every glass ceiling in sight.

"Let me run this up your flagpole, see if it raises any sort of salute. You lot over at No.11 are all for not having to spend your money and making it for HMRC, yah?"

"Yah."

"What would you say to a chance to cut several million a year on expenditure and make...?"

"What?" Catriona was almost panting. This was the stuff to interest women these days, far more than sex.

"Well, I was going to say 'a killing' on the old Inheritance Tax but it sounded not quite right."

"I'm all ears- and that's a figure of speech. Not a selfie."

"If I said, 'de Coverlet' to you, what would you do?"

"Laugh probably. The only de Coverlet I know is Philip- I was going to say he 'works for the FO' but 'work' really doesn't do justice to his ah- involvement. Is that who you mean?"

"Well, it must be the same family but... it seems... that there is every possibility... that this cousin of his... ah." He consulted his notes unnecessarily- this name had been seared into his head ever since he had first been given the job. "Ah- Cosmo." And here he leant even closer, despite the fact that there was no-one else in the room, "Could well be the real King of at least England. And possibly all the other bits too...!"

What this unspeakable product of political aspiration did not know, along with almost everybody except for the de Coverlets' close family and, inevitably, the many generations of Hives, was that under that Endowment Coffer, in the Endowment Room, was another rather incongruous, dusty box, not an obvious support for a coffer. If one had been forced to describe its shape, 'coffin' might have been offered after one or two more likely attempts and this would have been right. There were words carved into the corner of the lid but as they were apparently in Latin, and even at the best of times, very few had been able to read, let alone understand it- they were almost illegible. One word stood out from the rest of the script and that was 'rex' and most of those who did think about it felt that it might be rather an opulent resting place for a family pet. The other words ' quondam' and 'futurus' were virtually illegible and of little interest to any but the guardians of the box. For within, indeed, lay the body of *rex quondam, rexque futurus,* the once and future king. King Arthur.

Now, just about every part of Britain and it seems, other countries too, claim Arthur as theirs and most have a legend of him waiting with his knights beneath the earth for the moment when they would awaken and ride forth in defence of the realm in its most dire predicament.

The fact that he has not as yet done so, proves either that the legend is not true or, as his staunch supporters maintain, not even the bombing of London in the Second World War was bad enough to summon him and that there must be worse to come.

Only the de Coverlets knew for sure that this event was unlikely as the old chap's bones had been lying in the Counting House ever since the house had been built around them and had indeed, been somewhere in the environs almost ever since the Last Battle at Camlann, 1500 years ago. This story has rarely been told.

Chapter Eleven

We learn that the Last Battle between Arthur and his bastard son, Mordred, took place on the River Cam, or Camel, not far from present-day Wadebridge. Arthur won but was fatally wounded. But what few knew was that a distant relative of Jago, simply known as Ocken, had had similar aspirations to Jago in a desire to see the world. At a time when crossing the nearby River Fowey was rare and the Tamar undreamt of, Ocken had heard of a whole new world in Ireland. It was there that the beautiful Yseut had been born and from there that steady stream of rather earnest and smelly pilgrims had started to come through the Duchy on the way to Rome. Ocken, being Cornish and capricious decided to go against the flow and had followed what is now called the Saints' Way' (a name given to it by its users) and had made it past the ford at Wadebridge and was fishing out of Padstow, where he had picked up a little craft that he could handle himself with a pair of oars and a lugsail. And when the news came down the river that they'd had a battle and that there was need for a boat to take some posh nob and his attendants out west, Ocken thought: Well, I'm goin' back 'ome d'reckly; might as well see if I can't pick up a couple of quid along the way." (Of course, all this was in Cornish as very few had the Latin and none the Anglo-Saxon).

So he offered and was surprised to see three ladies, all dressed in black, arriving on the quay just where Rick Stein has got his Seafood Restaurant now, who managed to clamber aboard. Now, long black frocks are not the best clothing for boarding 20-foot luggers from the shore. They didn't have ladders nor anything back then. Ocken offered to pick them up and deposit them personally and when this was refused, he was told to avert his eyes whereupon there was much rustling of underclothes- he recognised the sound from elsewhere- and the occasional glimpse of thigh- his experience of this was from a similar source- and eventually the three ladies were on board.

"Where to? Trip round the bay or do you fancy an afternoon mackerelling?"

"Just shut up," said the tallest, with a definite accent. "and do as you're told. To the battlefield."

So they sailed solemnly back up on the top of the tide, three ladies standing because they couldn't face sitting on Ocken's seats and were met by the victorious army.

"Blimey." thought Ocken," If these was the winners, I hates to think what the losers must look like!"

But then he looked a little closer and saw.

However, those battered knights who could stand, even if they were missing a limb or two, carried a stretcher on board and laid it on a couple of up-turned crab pots, covered with an ermine cloak.

"All ashore who's going ashore!" called Ocken, trying to introduce a little levity into the occasion but it wasn't every day that the King of the Britons passes away, so he was ignored.

"If we'm gonna catch the tide...! Us'll 'ave to shake a leg."

Slowly and majestically the boat slid towards the sea, the three ladies standing, their hooded heads bowed in black veils over the pall making a memorable image for those who saw it and were capable of any recall.

"Sorry to interrupt and that, but I've got to know where we'm goin'. If an' I'm gonna steer."

The middle queen, for indeed queens they were, Morgan La fey, the Queen of Northgalis, or North Wales and the elderly Queen of the Wastelands, said something which he didn't understand.

Morgan explained: "She's Welsh."

"Thought us Cornish was supposed to understand they."

"North Wales. Not even the Welsh can understand them. Cause of many rifts in early Christian doctrine."

"Yeah, but where? For a start, left or right?" They had reached the mouth of river where the famous Doom Bar loomed to starboard and the rock menaced them ahead.

"But to the Islands of the Dead, of course."

"The Islands of the Dead!!??"

Ocken, like every child brought up in Cornwall knew that, out beyond Penn an Wlas were the Islands of the Dead, the last vestiges of the ancient land of Atlantis and the few who could afford it were taken there to await Armageddon; however, sixteen miles in an open boat with three old ladies and a stiff was not Ocken's idea of a pleasure cruise. Be that as it may, he did turn left where the river met the sea and let the ebbing tide draw them to the West, past the beaches and then the cliffs as they neared the end of the world.

The old ladies had long before abandoned their opposition to the scaly benches; indeed, the old Queen of the Northgalis had completely discarded all pretence of regal majesty and was lying beside Arthur, vomiting into an old bucket. Morgan and the Queen of the Wastelands were arguing about the efficacy of their sort of magic when faced by that of Nature.

"I never said I could control the weather," said Morgan. "It's more a matter of persuading the people that what we get was what I prophesied."

"And what are you prophesying?"

And before the great necromancer could reply, Ocken butted in: "From the look of that lot ahead, out to the North West, a right old load o' shite."

His meteorological observations were spot on. The old Welsh queen was begging to be put out of her misery; the Queen of the Wastelands had given up the pretence of tending to her companion and was throwing up overboard, once Ocken has shown her which side to use and one of Morgan la Fey's closest secrets was revealed when she could not help vomiting her skilfully-tooled dentures into the spume-flecked waters of the Atlantic Ocean.

"Now let's see your magic get they back." thought Ocken to himself.

"But is there nothing you can do to help us?" Morgan

pleaded, wiping the specks from the corner of her mouth.

"Yais!" said Ocken happily," But not if you wants to go out West with yon carcass. If we turns round and runs fer it, up East, into the Mouse Hole, all 'd be tickedy boo." It was a phrase he had heard but never used before.

To cut a long story short, that was what they did; rounded Land's End and ran up the south coast. Ocken left three very bedraggled old queens standing on the sand in the Mouse Hole, a very handy little bight that offered some protection from the storm and headed happily on back up the coast towards home. Unluckily for him, the weather did take a turn for the worse just as he was approaching his own cove and the boat overturned, throwing both Ocken and the box into the sea. Ocken, like most seafarers down the ages, had never learned to swim, on the very sound logic that it only put off the drowning which you might well have got on with, and as he was going down for the third time, he felt the side of the coffin pushing him towards the shore and safety. There did seem to be some sort of intent within and he went with the flow.

Ocken dragged the box on to the sand of the foreshore and was just able to mutter to the youngsters gathering around: "You touch that box and I'll fillet yer bollocks and shove 'em up your arse" before he passed out. Ocken's knifemanship was so well known that, when he came round, no-one had touched him or the coffin, which he had dragged to his hovel and where it remained for the next several centuries.

Quite how it came to be kept in the Endowment Room

at Mena Dhu is lost in time. Once the family had decided what they had got, yet another clause was added to the Oath of Silence that every senior member of the family was made to swear as soon as they were old enough to understand the importance of what they had learnt. There were some who were never bothered with the oath, in that they could hardly dress themselves, let alone keep secrets upon which the security of the nation, later the Empire and ultimately the Commonwealth depended. It was up to whichever of the Hives family was in service at the time to keep the brighter members of the Hockings well supplied with whatever was their poison, so that memories of the box and what it might contain disappeared somewhere in the Eighteenth Century.

In a new bistro in Campden Passage in London, the two conspirators were deep in conversation over the speciality, onglet steak and beetroot.

"Her Maj- when I say: her Maj, I don't just mean, like, an equerry. I mean, like, in person, gives it to him. He actually comes up from Buga-Buga land to the big city to tea and saffron cake- it's what they eat down there- and takes the Coutts cheque away with him. If they ever learned about BACS or CHAPS, they wouldn't even have to do that, but I think they both enjoy the social side. She pays him two million quid every year just to do nothing, like, stay cool, not rock the boat, no whispering about the bloodline. Waste him, that's £2 million saved as a starter. If he stays unwed and... 'unproductive', shall we say- AND we can take out cousin Philip at the same time."

"Well, that's no bother. The man's a walking disaster waiting to happen. He's off to Mongolia next. He could easily lose himself there. With a little help"

Catriona wasn't joking.

"Brill- so, wipe out the line- sad, maybe. But the death duties on their estates would be billions."

"The King of England?!"

Out on Bodmin Moor, Cyril Oliphant was having a problem getting the concept through to Auroch and Gaia, who had been christened Brian and Tina respectively, in suburban Erdington some 30 years previously.

"And possibly Wales and Scotland as well, though I'm not so sure about that."

"An' what d'yow want us to do?"

"Well, I thought, kidnap him..."

"Fer munay?"

"Oh yes- that's the usual thing, isn't it?"

"'Ow much?"

"I'm not quite sure about that yet, I mean, how much would you pay for the rightful King of England?"

"Millions." said Auroch.

"At least," said Gaia, and scratched her armpit.

"Well, I rather agree with you and I know exactly where and when, if you're on."

"Jus' a minit-" Gaia seemed to be nearer to reality than her partner whose head was usually in a cloud of strange-smelling smoke. "Wot's the split?"

"Split? Is that some new slang...?"

"Naow! The split. How do we- you an'... us- split the munay?"

"Oh, I see." Cosmo hadn't thought of the finer financial details. "I'm really not interested in the money- munnay- it's more of a... philosophical thing-"

"Philosophy's cack!" This was Auroch's contribution to the discussion.

Chapter Twelve

Hidden in the mass of trees that surround Mena Dhu is a green jewel: a sixty-yard perfect circle of grass, the de Coverlet cricket field. True, there may be more magnificent settings for the ancient game- Lord's, of course; some say Arundel Castle, or one of the Australian concrete basins, or Indian termite nests of hysteria but for the peaceful contemplation of the beautiful game, this is a Bach prelude as opposed to Black Sabbath. It is the pride and joy of the gardener, Abel Tonkin.

Few knew it but Abel Tonkin was not just employed to oversee the gardens and woodlands that made up the estate at Mena Dhu; he had been employed by the current Master of the House's father, old Lord Cosmo, currently percolating in a darkened room, because, as a young man, he had been on the ground staff at Lord's and so his knowledge of the preparation of cricket pitches had been handed down from the Highest of the High.

For the uninitiated, this, for the cricket-pitch producer, is the equivalent of the Cambridge tripos or the SAS course at Hereford. Understandably, for once, the Australians give their groundsmen the credit they are due and call them 'curators'!

He was discussing the Big House's possible team with Hives and Cosmo and was bemoaning the lot of the game, both locally and nationally. There was a time, quite recently, within the last twenty years, when Porthwallow had produced not one but two cricket teams; they had wafted around the lower Cornish leagues, the firsts usually a league or two about the second XI who had, for three years solidly, ended each season bottom of Cornwall Division 2 East, arguably the worst team in the county, if not the West of England. In the end, those senior players, who had numbered Jago Hocking and Hezekiah Pemberthy when they weren't fishing, amongst the few, had decided that it was a waste of time, driving all the way to Bude, for instance with eight players, three of them under fourteen from the local community college, the acolytes of the PE teacher who was a keen cricketer, only to get stuffed by some big-headed prat, miffed at being dropped from the firsts who insisted on opening the bowling and the batting, bowled fifteen of the thirty overs allocated and then knocked off the runs in half the time available. He did not realize that it was not his ability that kept him out of the firsts but his attitude. Not even the tremendous match teas, where the wives, sweethearts and mothers of the home teams competed even more zealously than their men-folk in handicapping the visitors with an excess of scones, lardy cake, saffron buns, sausage rolls and small pasties, not even these could make up for the regular season's results of played 12, lost 11, one abandoned due to high winds which kept blowing the bails off.

"What about this PE chappie?" asked Cosmo. "Could we get him?"

"Sadly, no," replied Abel. "They built a Sports Hall over

his cricket pitch, which nobody ever uses on a Saturday, except for a few ladies playing badminton so he buggered off to somewhere where they still play the game- Australia, I think."

"But it wasn't that long ago that we were winning the Ashes and the whole country was behind the team." said Lord de Coverlet. "Remember that open top bus ride round London, Freddy Flintoff and Pietersen, pissed as farts? The whole country cheered because they were on the BBC television! Everyone watched that last afternoon at Lord's. But now, if it wasn't for dear old TMS, I wouldn't even know who was playing- never see them on telly."

"Sky, milord." said Abel. "They'm buyin' everything. Soon only thing left on the BBC'll be the Boat Race, Crufts and tiddlywinks!"

"Well, just make sure that Boots, what's his name- Salt- make sure he can hold up an end."

"Ais, milord" said the groundsman. "As you wasn't usin' it, I cut a wicket on the tennis court, help to brush up his game all round. And introduce the Poles, just in case."

Even here, in the mystic woodlands of Mena Dhu, Eastern Europeans who gladly laboured at those jobs that the indigenous would, or could not do, had appeared. There were two, almost silent, at best monosyllabic Poles, Aleksy and Felicks, but it meant that the undergrowth was kept under more control than it had been since before the First War, when the army of gardeners who were employed then had all joined up together and marched off to the Front, never to return.

Much of his work from April onwards was done on the cricket ground, nay, on the cricket pitch itself and when his Lordship commented on some other part of the estate being even more unkempt than usual, Abel would explain it away by saying he was working on the pitch. When he was questioned as to whether the lad might do the thinning, Abel explained that; "'e's larnin'. Can't start early enough larnin' about pitches."

Cosmo and his father, when *compos mentis,* had agreed to spending thousands on the latest little tractors, Dennis mowers and ganging machines, white-line painters and movable sight-screens- whatever Tonkin had asked for- but when he had been offered the chance to buy the latest gadget for actually marking the creases, Abel had refused in favour of his strip of 3" by 2" timber, a bucket of whitewash and a paintbrush.

"I'd never trust no machine ter do it proper" he explained.

"Hives?"

The phone had rung in the spectacular hallway at Mena Dhu and Hives shimmied down the great staircase.

Though not an excessively imaginative man, Hives could not avoid the memory of the staircase in the 'Masquerade' scene in 'The Phantom of the Opera' and if he was sure no-one was watching, he would indulge in a flex kick or two and there.

"Mena Dhu?"

"Hawkins here, Hives" The old Admiral still bellowed as if he were in a storm off Murmansk. "Is Cosmo free for a word?"

"Ah, your Lordship." Even though he was no longer

Admiral of the Fleet, he was still a Lord, which made it a bit difficult, "I am sure that his Lordship would be very pleased to speak with you. If you wouldn't mind waiting a moment, I shall endeavour to find him."

De Coverlet was in his counting house; while he attempted to hide the fact, he was in truth a very accomplished book keeper, something which his *de facto* accountant recognised and even, occasionally, not entirely jokingly, offered him a job. He was keeping an eye on some of the easier investments.

"I am not sure that we should be keeping quite so much in Renewables. I'm all for saving the planet but we do have to generate income as well as cheap electricity."

"Excuse me sir, but we have Admiral Hawkins on the telephone. If you would like to raise that handset?"

Cosmo remembered the Admiral's usual tone and so held the receiver a little way from his ear before pressing the appropriate button. "Bobby? How nice to hear you."

"Likewise, I'm sure." Never one for small talk, the Admiral got to the point. "Now. Cosmo, d'you remember Izzy?"

"I'm not..."

"Little Izzy? One of my tribe. Adam's little girl. You won't have seen her for years."

"Ah, well, then..." Cosmo was racking his brains. He was not particularly fond of others' progeny and the Admiral had so many grandchildren.

"Probably at my seventieth. We did manage to wheedle you over on that occasion, I seem to remember..."

"Yes. Splendid do." Cosmo hated social occasions with more than a tableful of people. A big table, possibly, like the one in Mena Dhu's dining room which could seat twenty four at full stretch but one at which you were guaranteed a seat, preferably at the head; those does where you were supposed to act like a Neapolitan acrobat and juggle a glass of wine, a plate of indeterminate food which really needed a knife and fork, among crowds of strangers with no shared interest and, if you were lucky, find a perch on a stair somewhere were anathema. Add to this a permanent undercurrent of small children at waist height and you had Sir Cosmo's idea of purgatory.

"There were quite a few grandchildren. "

"Ah, not all mine. Emma kept an open house and they were all allowed to bring friends, as long as they didn't mind sleeping in the same bed. Anyway. No. What I was trying to say was she's here. Splendid girl- joined the WRENS- family business, sort of. But she remembers you."

"That's jolly kind..."

"Something about a security breach on the lower decks."

"I beg your...?"

"It seemed you'd left your flies undone and for a sensitive little girl, it seems to have made quite an impression on her. Their heads are about crutch-height at that age, don't you know?"

"Oh, my word," Even down the phone, Cosmo blushed. "How awful. I hope nobody thought... or thinks...!"

"No, no. She said she just thought it was rather sad you

didn't have a mummy to help you get dressed."

"Just a minute." His thoughts were focussing. "Glasses. And a vast fabrication of ironwork in her mouth? Is that the one?"

"That's the one- her mother insisted on the orthodontals but I don't know how necessary it was. She always seemed a very pretty little girl to me. Still, thing is, doing what she does now, she's got to do a bit of exercise, even on leave, and she was wondering if she could paddle over and see you."

"Paddle? It's hardly paddling."

"She has one of these things she calls a kayak. Now," said the Admiral, who knew his boats, "as far as I'm concerned, a 'kayak' is the craft the Inuit used to use when I was on secondment to the Canooks- made out of seal skin, stank of fish but what does an old fart like me know. Izzy's is bright yellow plastic. Still, she does shift in it. I thought she might pootle across the bay over to you and if she's too knackered to paddle back, we could send a car, but she is surprisingly strong and a determined little missy. Takes after her mother. And grand-mama, for that matter. So, if it's all right with you, don't be surprised if she surfaces your side. Looking forward to the cricket- young Bobby's a bit of a star, don't you know? Glad you've got him on our side. I'll see you there, then." With which, he rang off before Cosmo had any chance to refuse hospitality.

"Hives," he said to the butler who was standing at his side. "It seems that we are to have a visitor. A young lady, though exactly how and when I'm not sure. Do we have any of that Coca Cola stuff? It's what these young people drink, isn't it?"

"I believe so, somewhere, but the Admiral's seventieth was nearly twenty years ago, sir. Do you we know how young this young lady might be?

"Oh," said his Lordship. "I hadn't thought of that."

The kayak, seen from Cosmo's hiding place on the edge of the woods around the big house, looked like a bright insect, a waterboatman with a different rig, or a very determined bee, in that it headed straight for the cliff below Mena Dhu.

"How far is that, Hives? Across the estuary?"

"I am not sure, Sir Cosmo but it must be at least two miles."

"Not bad in a canoe."

"No, sir."

"How do you think she intends getting from the water's edge up to the house? We can hardly send her a car. Drop a rope, I suppose."

"No, sir."

"Best keep an eye on her."

"Yes, sir."

"I mean, even if she can find her way into the Cove, that path up only gets used by the occasional idiot wanting a swim and I can't remember the last time we had cousin Philip to stay."

Eventually, the black-clad figure on the yellow craft disappeared from view beneath the cliff.

"D'you think we ought to have some of that... CCTV stuff

installed down there, Hives?"

"It's a possibility, sir but is it worth the expense?"

"Well, if we're going have all these self-propelled young ladies discovering the cove, there could be a real danger of beach parties."

"Indeed, sir."

"And one wouldn't want to miss one of those. Ssh! Can you hear her? Should be here by now."

The master of the House and his butler were standing at the head of the path, peering down, listening intently for any sound from the overgrown dirt path, when a throat was cleared behind them.

"Excuse me."

They swung round, expecting a maid or something, only to see a strangely conglomerated person. Clad in the what was becoming the ubiquitous seaside *'ensemble'* of a black wet suit was what appeared to be a cherubic tadpole. The person- and the contours displayed by the unflattering suit led both the onlookers to believe it to be female- was not tall, and against the six-foot Hives appeared positively short, but this immediately predisposed Sir Cosmo to their visitor, as he was not much above five-foot six. She took off the neoprene cap which had been covering her head to reveal a golden head of hair, cut *'a la gamine'*.

At second sight, she was not the child she had appeared to be. There were wrinkles which most women spent thousands of pounds trying to remove; her nose had indeed been broken but mended with expert no-expense-spared care; and the hair-thin white crease that followed her laugh-line down one cheek was not matched by one on the other. But she had the most opal-blue, jewel-bright eyes that Cosmo had ever seen.

"I know this is going to sound silly, "she chuckled in a warm gurgle, "But I'm not even sure which of you is my host- if either. The last time I saw Sir Cosmo it wasn't so much his face I was focusing on as... lower down."

"Ah, well, yes- that'll have been me. Forgetful. And you must be the Admiral's little Izzy?"

"Yes, I-"

"Excuse me, Miss." It was Hives. "I am most sorry to be interrupting but how did you get here? We know about your little boat- but you weren't on the path- we'd have seen you."

"Ah, no- I hope you don't mind- I set myself a challenge- to see if I could free climb Mena Dhu cliff. I didn't have any talc but it wasn't that hard- not when you've got hands like mine." And on the end of her arms, the strength of which was hinted at through the wetsuit, where there should have been soft white hands were, quite honestly, claws. The nails were worn flat, the pads at the tips of her fingers like old leather, the fingers steely clamps and the palms like the soles of most people's feet.

"Consequence of what we use them for, I'm afraid." And, enigmatically, she left it at that.

It would have been impolite of either of the men to ask the questions that they were both dying to and so Hives fell back on a trusted standard.

"Would you care for some tea, Miss?"

"Love a cup, Hives. I presume you are Hives? Uncle Bobby gave me a pretty specific description."

"Yes, Miss. Out here or..." He looked rather disapprovingly at her wet suit.

"Out here will be fine. I could take this lot off, but I've not got much on underneath. Nothing suitable for the lofty towers of Mena Dhu."

"Oh, we're very informal here." replied Cosmo, as his butler went in search of suitable crockery for an *al fresco* tea. "In fact, I myself used to be seen quite frequently disporting myself in little more than my kilt. Though no so often these days."

"Well, if you'll just give me a hand with this cord here"- she pointed to a lanyard hanging down." It can be done single-handed but, like most things, it's more fun with two."

Cosmo pulled on the cord, there was a velcro-ripping noise and Izzy began to unpeel from the neck down. She stopped at her waist, revealing muscled shoulders, a very neat bust, properly clad in a black sports bra and an impressive six-pack. Cosmo viewed the revelation with an expert eye and noted a fairly vivid scar, low down, to the right.

"Appendix?" he offered.

"AK47." she replied. "One of ours, too. Those chaps do fire off at the slightest opportunity- into the air, I know- but they never think about where they're going to land."

They moved over to sit on the patio, awaiting their tea.

Cosmo tried another tack.

"Izzy? That must be short for something- Isobel?"

"Nothing so straightforward in our family. No, my parents had two major passions, apart from a mutual one for each other- Cornwall and Opera. Now there aren't many works that satisfied both. 'Pirates of Penzance' of course, and 'Tristan and Isolde'. And they really wanted to name their child after one of the characters. If I'd have been a boy, I could have been either Mark or even Tristan, a Frederic or at a push, Stanley, but sadly I limited their choice by appearing without appendages. If it was to be from 'Pirates,' the choice was Mabel or Edith and I believe there was an Aunt Edith, somewhere in the family, whom no-one liked, so they had to revert to the Wagner."

"Isolde?!" exclaimed Sir Cosmo.

"I'm afraid so-"

"But that's magnificent. I say, you're not married or anything, are you?"

She held out her battered, ringless hands. "Not anything, no."

"Excuse the impertinence but... er ... I don't quite know how to put this ... you're not... 'sapphic', are you?"

"What a strange question. I've never heard it put that way but, no- I don't bat for the other side."

"Talking of which," said Cosmo, getting more and more exited. "Do you play cricket? Would you like a game?"

At which point, Monica, the little maid appeared with a gigantic silver tray, bearing tea pot, cups, jugs of hot water and milk, slices of lemon, sugar, and a plate of immaculate cucumber sandwiches, on brown, crustless bread.

After a pleasant hour's chat, Izzy excused herself, citing a need to catch the tide to help her return to Porthwallow. She refused Cosmo's offer of accompanying her down the path to the cove, which secretly pleased him as he was not sure that he'd be able to make it back up again and, promising to see her at the match, he and Hives waved her out of sight down the path, whereupon the Master of the House turned to his butler and said:

"That, Hives, old chap, is the lady I shall marry."

Chapter Thirteen

⮑

"These old families, I mean, do we really need them? Hate to say it, but I think the Frogs got it just about right. Ok, so these de Coverlets- even sound French- they're not obvious candidates for the guillotine- it would be all rather too public. We'd have all sorts of preservation societies up in arms- I mean, if they can stop boats anchoring in Studland Bay for fear of hurting the bloody sea horses... I mean!"

Mark Tregaskis was in lycra, ready for the gym. A sweat band around his head, and a pair of serious knee braces proved that he was keen to show his commitment to fitness. More and more of the senior Civil Servants were abandoning the late-night wine-bar for the early morning gym, at least a few times a week. Catriona was more of a swimmer but their club had a pool as well as a gym.

"Look, Mark, must rush. I need to get fifty lengths in before the office opens at seven but we could touch base over lunch? Just mustn't give my James- or your lassie- any grounds for jealousy!"

"Who's next on your check list, Hives?"

It had been the local doctor, Morris Campbell, who had told Cosmo about risk assessment and event management, as much to get himself an invitation to play as due to worry about potential danger. He was the sort of cricket fanatic who kept his cricket gear in his car, just in case. If there was a medical emergency, he would have to fetch his medicine bag from the practice or from home but if there was the prospect of a game of cricket, he was ready. Some Saturdays, he would cruise the byways and cricket grounds of mid-Cornwall, ready to offer himself in case anyone, of no matter what hue, was short of a player. He regularly visited the old Lord in his coma, even if it was only to sign for the latest batch of medications that were flushed daily through the living remains of the old man and when he heard of the game, he struck.

"I can always be the first aid presence- you'll need that and will save on the cost of the St John's Ambulance- and I'd be glad to make up the numbers if you're short."

Cosmo knew that they did not have enough players and that Morris would kill two birds, but he did hesitate briefly because Morris Campbell was one of the most boring men he knew, and in his confined social circle, he knew some pretty boring people. He bit the bullet.

"Thanks, doc- that'd be great," whereupon he was handed a sheet of paper.

"I don't know if you've seen this sort of thing. Government are getting a bit hot on this risk assessment. Can't do a sodding thing about much but they're at least trying to keep A and E numbers down by advising the public not to trip over electric cables or slip on spilled beer. Trouble is, the sort of morons we've got these days, such warnings are necessary. The number of idiots we get demanding to be cleaned up because they'd checked to see if the sign WET PAINT still applied is incredible. And we did have a visitor from Bootle once, stuck his fingers in an electric socket to see if the thing was live."

So Hives and Sir Cosmo were going through the process with ever-increasing incredulity.

"Crowd control."

"Will there be a crowd?"

"Probably. Especially if Michael Donohoe is playing- he is a rock star, after all."

"Yes, one does forget such things- specially when he's such a pleasant quiet chap in himself."

"Should I have a word with Bert Drake at the cop shop? He is the fount of all things legal. And he enjoys his cricket. Remember? When the village still had a team?"

"Well, at least he'll know one end of a bat from another, which is more than can be said for our two Poles. Though, if we put one in each team, it should balance things out."

"Poles apart, you mean, my lord?" said Hives, unable to restrain a slight snigger.

"I was wondering who would succumb to the temptation," said Sir Cosmo with a melodramatic sigh.

At a garden table of a pub on the edge of Wimbledon Common, Tregaskis was buying a bottle of Kirin Ichiban for a man who appeared incapable of smiling. Immaculate in black, his silk shirt buttoned to the neck, his face that of a male model if it had not been for the scars, he kept his conversation brief.

"Well?"

"Like I said, how much?"

"Is this solo or do I need to bring in my team?"

"Depends how you do it. I don't want to know details."

"Why me?"

"Well, we were at University together, for a start."

"Till I got kicked out- or what is it they call it? 'Sent down'! Arrogant pricks."

"Well, I think they were quite fond of the college cat."

"Should never have bit me."

"But that's neither here nor there. We could make this official but I'd rather the fewer people knew about it the better."

"So this is private. Not on the NHS?"

"You could put it that way."

"So you have to pay."

"Like, I said. How much?"

And so it was, on a beautiful Saturday in early September, the summer reluctant to surrender its lease, that the two teams met at the Mena Dhu ground.

The MCC would not necessarily have approved of all the kit but the tradition of (predominantly) white was maintained. On the one side, his Lordship, Hives, the doctor, Bobby Hawkins and Abel Tonkin were wearing full, immaculate whites and a variety of sleeveless sweaters in the colours of various prestigious clubs which only Abel recognised. He had even managed to fit out the boy, Salt, in some old, moth-eaten flannels, kept up- in the time-honoured manner- by a club tie, and a proper shirt. He had refused to let him wear a t-shirt, not even one boasting the iconic Batman symbol, "An' anyway, tis Bat S man." PC Drake had discovered that, somehow, his cricketing gear must have shrunk in the wash, as he could get neither the shirt nor the trousers around his waist.

"I s'll 'ave to 'ave a word with the missus. Must've been washin' 'em too 'ot." He wore jeans, his only casual option, as did both of the Poles.

Cousin Philip was down, before being sent away again; and he had decided that he was a shooting brake for the occasion, a cream one but it did mean that he was wearing brown brogues.

Cosmo, smitten as he was with Izzy, had ordered Mrs Walker to provide the ladies who were going to play with a dressing room of some description. Remembering Hunt Balls as the only occasion on which such accommodation had been arranged, she applied her mind and her imagination.

"Abel?" she asked of the gardener at breakfast one morning, "could you and the lads get the old gypsy caravan across to the ground for match day? And could young Tom give it a lick of paint? Pink, I think."

Abel could not think of any reason to refuse and so Edie

Walker, being ignorant of cricket matches and thinking more of the Hunt Balls that she had attended, produced a sort of boudoir on wheels, complete with a discrete commode behind a Japanese screen, a bucket in lieu of a bidet, with two mirrored dressing tables, topped off with powder puffs, quick wipes, smelling salts, tampons and a couple of considerate condoms. She obviously did not know the ladies for whom this was being provided. Tegan and Izzy had both ridden up with Bobby and the Admiral, both in all-enveloping tracksuits, each with a little rucksack. They had met before, obviously and so had chatted away in the back while Bobby drove and the Admiral boomed.

For a moment, Izzy glanced away from her fellow, her eye caught by the sight of someone in the crowd.

"What the-?" she started.

"Something the matter?" asked Tegan.

"I thought... No. It's just, I thought I recognised someone, but he couldn't be..."

And she returned her attention to the matter in hand.

Having been prepared to change 'round the back', they were most amused by their gypsy caravan, they had hooted with laughter at what they had been afforded and emerged, each stunning in her own specific way. Tegan was hiding her light beneath a great, sloppy white sweater that Bobby had lent her, but nothing could hide her lycra-clad legs once she took off her tracksuit bottoms. But Izzy, if anything, surpassed her as she came down the steps in a simple white polo shirt and white gymnastic shorts, long socks and white suede boots, nothing outdoing her sun-burnished thighs and forearms.

In the village's team, both Jeremy and the Vicar wore cream flannels which they were quietly delighted to see still fit. Michael was also all in white but the style was more Alexander McQueen than Lord's. Jake, who had been allowed to play, wore a white t-shirt and a white baseball cap, backwards, with the logo of his Little league team covered by a badge that he and Sandy had concocted together, with the letters PCC, for Porthwallow Cricket Club, emblazoned across it. For the rest, they had either grey flannels or jogging bottoms and a variety of white shirts, some of which were normally reserved for births, deaths and marriages. Few wore proper cricket boots but as the design of the professionals' gear had gradually moved from the leather nailed boot to the rubber-bottomed trainer, so the collection of footwear on display was not too galling to Abel, the perfectionist.

Sir Cosmo, of course, was to captain the Mena Dhu team, while Jago Hocking had the definite honour of leading the Porthwallow men (boy and Tegan). Jago remembered all too well how, in the past, despite all intention of abstaining, they had been overcome by the delights of Cook's match teas and that it had been agony to try to bowl and field after, so when Cosmo had tossed the 1933 penny he kept for such occasions, Jago had called Heads and been delighted to win, not hesitating to put the Big House in to bat.

A large crowd- for Mena Dhu- had taken what space they

could around the boundary, the determination with which they had fought for room for their rugs being almost Germanic. They were prepared for an enjoyable afternoon and there was little inter-team hostility because they felt that they belonged to both sides. And vice versa. And there was free beer.

Jago kept wicket. Hezekiah was to bowl the first over. The Vicar and his partner stood in the Slips. Michael and Jake patrolled the leg side, roughly at Midwicket, while Tegan, looking magnificent, filled the role of what has come to be called the 'boundary runner' or 'the off-side sweeper'- a term from Association Football but which purists still prefer to call Deep Extra Cover. Steve, the farmer, stood in the Gulley, Alf, the milkman, at Mid Off, Nathan, who was to bowl the second over was at Long Leg while Felicks, the Polish labourer, had been put by Jago at long stop and been told to stop what balls came anywhere near him, to catch it if he could and to throw it hard back to Jago.

And a real and affectionate roar went up when the young-ish Lord of the Manor, arguably next in line to the throne of England, and his butler walked to the wicket. In days gone by, the lord had played the shots and the butler done the running for him but now emancipation was such that they batted together and ran, albeit always in reply to the lord's call.

Sir Cosmo was to face the first ball which, without moving his feet, he dispatched over the toiling H.'s head for a straight six. The next was pulled backward of square for four. The third, a flighty slice for six over an absent Third man and the fourth straight past Alf for four. Even Jake had stopped calling "Go, H., go, H.!" before each ball and no-one was sure where the next might land.

"Right", said H. as he marched past the umpire back to his mark. "That's enough fuckin' deference!" The next was a bouncer; Cosmo had already proved with the third ball that he was not so secure with them up round his ears and again he flailed wildly at this one, got a top edge and it sailed skywards, high over Jago's head, heading for an unlikely six over the Long Stop boundary. However, Felicks, as directed, caught it perfectly inside the rope and hurdled it back at Jago, who didn't.

Twenty for one in the first over with one ball left. Bobby, who had made a hundred at Lord's in the Eton-Harrow game and been pestered by various counties to come and play for them, all of which he had refused, strolled in.

There was no getting away from it: he would have been top of the list at Central Casting for remakes of anything from 'Lawrence of Arabia' to 'Notting Hill'. Although all the women were smitten and there was an audible moan from the crowd as he walked out, fortunately he was not aware of his looks. He knew that he was personable and the fact that Tegan has chosen him as her current squeeze- a role that was becoming ever more permanent- proved something but he was not sure what.

"One leg, please, sir."

It was the first time that Charlie Onions, landlord of *The de Coverlet Arms* who had taken the afternoon off to umpire, had been called 'sir' for a very long time.

"If that means 'Leg stump', lad, you got it."

Bobby stretched, touched the ground, ran on the spot and then settled. H. took a few extra steps backwards to extend his run and then ran. He hurled the ball at Bobby's legs with all his might.

Bobby touched it expertly out towards Tegan, called: "Come one, Hives" and they easily jogged the single needed to take Bobby to the other end, ready for the next over.

He continued to stroke Nathan and Hezekiah around, ensuring that they took the necessary single at the end of each over and by the end of the fourth, the score stood at 50 for one, with Bobby on 30 and Hives yet to score.

"'Tis time," Jago called. "Fight fire with fire, eh? C'mon, maid." And he threw the ball to Tegan. Slowly she walked from her fielding position, out in the deep, towards the stumps, all the while gazing knowingly at Bobby. Equally slowly and with equal mysterious intent, she stopped, looked at all her fielders and then, turning to Charlie, proceeded to remove her previously all-concealing sweater to reveal that the white lycra leggings were in fact only the lower part of an all-white, skin-tight one-piece sleeveless leotard.

"I say," said Bobby, the mildest of the expletives to be heard muttered all round the ground, by players and spectators alike. Again, though no-one mentioned it, it was obvious that the leotard was all that she needed to keep her magnificent chest under control, and when she stretched, prior to bowling, it was equally obvious that the leotard was having a considerable demand made of its construction to fulfil the role.

She paced out a reasonable run, nothing excessive and the first ball was little more than a loosener, which Bobby, being the gentleman he was, batted back to her.

"No need to be sarcastic," she called over her shoulder.

Taking this to be a declaration of war, Bobby planted the next through the stable door of the ladies' boutique boudoir caravan.

"Right," said Tegan, added several more strides to her run-up and imitating the action of a tigress, stiffened her sinews and raced in. Bobby smiled in anticipation but while he had been admiring the hypnotic motion of her bust, he had not noticed that she had changed her grip and the ball, instead of flying, came floating out of her hand. Bobby was through his shot before the ball was halfway down the pitch and rapped him on his pads, right in front of the wicket. The entire team, with the exception of Felicks who did not understand, yelled: "Howzat!" and Charlie could do nothing but raise his finger.

"Sorry, Master Bobby, but I never seen nothin' more plum in me life."

Bobby looked at Tegan.

"Well played. But the game is not over yet!"

Cosmo sent the doctor in next, mainly to avoid him boring the rest of those left in the pavilion. He poked about for three overs as if searching for an appendicitis, playing each ball with an immaculate forward defensive stroke. One or two balls manage to streak off the edge and Hives forced the doctor to run but not without an expression of disdain on his face. Eventually, in a further attempt to keep the score moving, Hives ran himself out.

Whereupon Philip de Coverlet abandoned his shooting brake persona and drove himself to the middle as an imaginary Morgan.

"Sporty little number, don't you know."

While the doctor continued with his cautionary defence, Philip proceeded to scythe wildly in a style that would have been anathema to his erstwhile coaches at Eton, more suited to the wet-bobs than the dry, but as they were all most likely dead and certainly none present, there was no real criticism. Abel Tonkin winced and looked away but it was not his place to criticize the aristocracy.

They did make a few runs, but what with the doctor's reluctance to leave his crease until the ball was past a fielder and Philip's need to call out his procedure of "Depress clutch, engage first, handbrake off, accelerate!" each time that they essayed a run, it meant that the scoring was rather slow.

Philip was out to the first straight ball that Michael managed to pitch. "First time I've played in nearly thirty years," he exclaimed modestly to his team mates but Jake broke the spell by adding: "Yeah, but we've been practising in the yard ever since we got the invite."

They sent the boy, Salt, in next, to try to accelerate the scoring but the only thing that accelerated was his heartbeat. The sight of Tegan, even off her short run, was too much for any red-blooded lad and he was physically incapable of keeping his eye on the ball when faced with so much peripheral distraction. He lobbed a simple return catch to her, a sort of votary's offering.

Abel was steaming on the boundary.

"What 'eve I bin teechin' fer this past month? Nice relaxed bat, take the pace off the ball! You'm clutchin' it like it was your... I don't know what!" He did know but was reluctant to say so in front of ladies.

"Well, you see if'n you can't do any better!" said the boy and threw his bat down, on the edge of tears.

"And what about that rule about only one bouncer in an over?" he returned. "She's got two, every ball!"

The doctor, used as he was to the female anatomy in all states, was not affected by Tegan. They needed someone to accompany him who was at least equally diffident. Then they realised that they had the ideal opponent- Izzy. She marched to the wicket in pads that nearly reached her waist, but the condescending amusement changed when she took a very professional guard and smote Tegan very correctly through the covers for four.

"Never doubted her," said the Admiral to Cosmo. "Can do just about anything, that girl."

And he wasn't far short of the mark. For a start, she removed the doctor. Prior to her arrival, his calling had consisted of: "Yes, sorry, no, listen, just a minute, sorry," thereby nearly removing several of his own team.

Izzy solved this by calling smartly, 'Yes' as she touched the ball straight to the milkman and in spite of her pads, she raced to the other end, before the doctor realised what was happening, namely both of them standing at the same end, but with him out of his ground. Alf did not even need to throw the ball to Jago behind the stumps; he simply walked and, rather sarcastically, removed the bails one by one.

The doctor had to go which he did, muttering something about "should never allow women to play- they don't understand the ethos of the game."

There then followed an amusing interlude when Aleksy, the Big House's Pole, came in to be greeted by a tirade of what was obviously jovial insult from Felicks, believing that no-one else could speak Polish. Unfortunately, Warsaw had been one of Cousin Philip's many, brief postings and he had been there long enough to pick up all the swear words- after all, isn't that what everybody always learns first, wherever they go?

So when "*Daj spokoj-Pokaż tym doopak, jak się bawić*" ("Come on, show these arseholes how to play") the cry of " *Kurvah mac!*" (roughly translated: "Fuck off!") was heard from the pavilion, and both Poles shut up.

Izzy had a very simple approach of batting with Aleksy. She told him; "If I say, Run, you run. If I say stay, you stay. Understood?"

"Yes, but please, miss, if you say nothing at all?"

"Just stay where you are."

Izzy managed to farm the bowling with as much success as her cousin had and gradually the score mounted. At the end of a fruitless over from a very sweaty H., the unholy trinity of Jago, H. and Nathan got together half way down the wicket.

"So, 'oo next? Tegan's 'ad 'er allocation and nobody'd believe us if we said we was bowlin' fer run-outs." Just then, a polite but intentionally audible cough was heard from the Vicar.

"You, Vicar?" asked H.

"No, no, no, no... but..." And he gave a violent nod sideways as if he had a terminal twitch, albeit in the direction of Jeremy, who was gazing intently at a blade of grass, as if he had never seen anything quite like it in his life.

"Would Jeremy-?"

"Well, if you insist," said the Vicar's friend, marching immediately towards Henry Lake, the shop keeper who was umpiring at the other end, having bravely entrusted the shop to his wife and two daughters. Henry regularly noticed that the consumption of ice cream and chocolate bars rose considerably whenever he was away, a rise totally unreflected in the takings in the till, but today he was going to let his pleasure at being involved in the cricket outweigh his fiscal anxiety. He had long since given up on his daughters' waistlines.

For the first time that afternoon, Jeremy removed his long-sleeved sweater, to reveal a sleeveless one, with a badge on the left breast pocket.

"Hey," said Henry, an ardent cricket fan, pointing to the

golden crown and white rose, and the blue trimming to the sweater. "A Hampshire badge. Who gave you that?"

"Hampshire," said Jeremy, quietly. "Only Twos, though."

With a cricket ball in his hand, Jeremy was transformed. He directed his fielders to exactly where they were wanted and ask Jago to stand up.

"You're not going to bowl wide, are you? I'm not very good when it's wide." confessed Jago.

Not many wicket keepers would admit to this almost universal truth.

"We'll see."

Aleksy was facing. Jeremy had a two step run-up and the ball appeared to be passing the Pole's backside by miles.

Before the thing had pitched, Izzy called: "Stay" but pitch it did, fizzed and took Aleksy's off bail like a kingfisher taking a minnow.

"Bugger me!" said Jago.

"That was better'n Warny's one against Fat Gatt!" said Henry, quoting a moment of golden cricket history.

"What he do?" asked Aleksy.

"Bowled you out!"

The pavilion was in uproar.

"I say- who is he?" asked Cosmo.

There were various answers.

"The Vicar's... friend."

"Partner."

"You know."

"Secretary to the Parish Council."

"And of the WI."

"Well, praise God, the art of leg spin bowling is alive and well and living in Porthwallow!"

Chapter Fourteen

Bert Drake, the local policeman and next man in, was getting nervous when he heard an all-too-well known voice.

"Out of uniform, Constable? I thought you were on duty?"

It was Inspector Foot, Bert's immediate superior and eternal anathema, in immaculate and very obvious dress uniform.

"I- I- I- I am, but I thought that if I played..."

"You're playing?! Dressed like that?!"

The fact that he was wearing cricket pads seemed to have passed the eagle-eyed sleuth by.

"His Lordship did ask me..."

Foot bridled at that, as an aspersion on his very existence.

"Was I not available?"

Bert did not know what to say, so he told the truth.

"He didn't ask."

"You mean, this irregular allocation of MY manpower went on without my knowledge or consultation? Where is this fellow? Lord or not, I-"

And he bristled even further.

Bert's honesty continued.

"He's standing right beside you." And he turned to the inconsequential-looking owner of the estate.

"Milord, I don't think you've met Inspector Foot. Come

down from the Met."

"Ah," said Cosmo, for indeed he had heard of this idiot and, revealing that ineffable capability that natural-born hosts display, said: "Foot of the Yard. Indeed, your reputation precedes you." He did not say what reputation. "Cricket your game?"

"Not exactly, your lordship. Du-did you say, my reputation?"

He was afraid of what this might be.

"Yes" said Cosmo, winging it. "Last time I saw Cressida, she was talking about you. Now, what was the problem here?"

"No, no- no problem. My idea, having... whatsisname?- Bert, here play- Community policing, you know. It is the latest initiative from... Cressida." It was the first time that he had ever used the first name of the Commissioner for the Metropolitan Police and it felt good!

"Carry on. Jolly good." And he tapped his cap with his leather-bound swagger stick, a move he had been practising in front of the mirror at home for ages.

"Thank you, milord," said Bert, under his breath, once the Inspector was out of sight.

"Looked as though you needed rescuing. As do we," he observed, as another cheer went up when Alistair, the postman, usually clad in Post Office red top and long shorts, winter and summer, having foregone his red for the day, Sunday, in exchange for a white polo shirt but retained his shorts, was bewildered by Jeremy's spin.

"How does he do that? How can anyone do that? "he wailed to the sky as he walked back to the pavilion.

Of course, Jeremy could not bowl from each end always and Jago felt that it was time for one of the true locals to oppose Bert, so called H. from his fielding position. He had arranged with Jago to field Long Leg one over and Long Off the other, which meant that he did not have to move much at all. Which meant that he had all but seized up. His opener nearly took Jago's head off, standing back. Charlie wasn't sure how to signal six wides and Felicks had not been expecting it either. As H. found his range, Bert plundered several runs and Izzy cover drove him for four which had those 'aficionados' in the crowd drooling.

"Could 'ave imagined that that were Gower." said one.

"If'n she were a bloke." added another. "And left-handed."

However, it only took two distracting balls of Tegan's final over to do for Bert. It was tradition that no-one bowled more than four, ever since the year when an ageing county bowler who was on holiday, persuaded the village to pick him then proceeded to bowl all ten overs from one end and then opened the batting. Old Sir Cosmo, young Sir Cosmo's father- had not been amused and returned several barrels of beer to the pub, unopened.

Which left Abel last man in, with Izzy at the other end, on 45, the score 125 for nine and two overs left, one to be bowled by Jeremy. Jago looked round his massed ranks, hoping for someone to step up and make the choice for him as to who would bowl the last.

"Dad, can I have a pitch?" Jake's voice could be heard all

round the ground, as intended.

"You'll have to ask Mr Jago," was an equally audible reply.

"Jake," asked Jago, "Do you know how to bowl, like the English?"

"Like Sir Francis Drake against the Spanish?"

"That wasn't quite what I meant. Um..."

"Like Sandy showed you, in the garden," said his father. "Not pitching at softball, but bowling a cricket ball?"

"Sure, pop- I mean, yes, dad." Michael was determined to eradicate the last few Americanisms from his son. The little figure strode in from the outfield, removed his baseball cap and handed it to Charlie.

"Is it right arm, lad?" the old man asked.

"Uh." Jake had to think for a minute. "Oh, sure."

"Right arm over," Charlie called to the serried ranks and stuck out his arm.

"No, sir. Charlie, sir, Sorry." It was Michael, who had come up to Mid Off to encourage his son.

"It's right arm. Under."

Such a call had not been heard in such a game for more than a hundred years. All conversation stopped. "Can I have the fielders on the edge, Mr Jago? 'Cepting Dad. And you, of course?"

Amused, Jago did as requested. Jake took no run up, simply two steps, and lobbed the ball high and slow. Abel couldn't believe it- it was actually coming out of the sun! Loath to offer the obvious heave that such a ball invited, he stood his ground and blocked it. The boo that went round the ground was humiliating. The next ball was equally high and if anything, even slower. He blocked it again and said: "What about the law that says you can't bowl more'n one ball above shoulder height?"

"That's after it's bounced, yer pillock," said H. who had gradually moved in closer as he saw the effect that they boy was having.

"Don't forget what Sandy showed you in the garden," Michael said to his son and made an arcane gesture with his right hand.

Abel, still chuntering, took his guard again, determined to show this young tacker a thing or two.

This time, the ball was nothing like so high but he could actually hear it rotating. He waltzed down the wicket, determined to plant it in the pavilion to show them but it pitched, bit and hissed past him, leaving him stranded. Unfortunately, it completely bamboozled Jago who missed the easiest stumping of his career and rolled slowly towards the boundary. And over it. Sadly, Felicks had taken that opportunity to answer a call of nature without telling anyone and was in the woods at the time.

"Sorry. I... piss." And he threw the ball back.

Abel was ready. This, like the previous, span viciously but he managed to hit it; in the air, towards the Vicar who had abandoned his post in the slips and been sent to patrol the covers. The Vicar went down on one knee, a much-performed action in church but this time, to form what is called the long barrier in the MCC's coaching manual as the correct way to stop a ball. However, this one did not stop spinning having been hit and it bounced and turned past Trevor who went sprawling; Abel called for a run. Izzy played out the rest of the over without distress.

The twentieth over- the Big House's last pair at the wicket, Jeremy, the Hampshire Second's alumnus versus Abel Tonkin, the erstwhile member of Lord's ground staff. Abel managed to hit the third and ran without thought. Izzy, summoning a voice reminiscent of her grandfather, the Admiral's at sea in a storm, called: "Stay!" after the one run and prepared to do what she could to finish the innings. But Jeremy was too good. Two dot balls, numbers four and five and a final heave from her which not only connected but also flew out of the ground. Very polite applause all round. 136 for 9, Izzy carrying her bat for 44 and admiration for Jake's lobs eclipsing Jeremy's remarkable performance.

It was while Tegan and Izzy had retired to their caravan to 'powder their noses' and Izzy was changing out of her bowling shorts into her batting shorts- apparently identical pairs of Navy issue, that Tegan saw the vivid scar on Izzy's thigh.

"Oh my God," she said. "How on earth...?"

"Ah," said Izzy, in a matter-of-fact manner, "a memento of my rape."

"Your what?!"

"Well, actually, something of an overstatement. He never quite succeeded. In Afghan... He'd threatened, and already got his *peshcabz* out-" Tegan looked bewildered; "His knife- and already done this so I played possum and while he was... distracted... unfastening- those dishdashas can be awkward, need both hands- I broke his neck."

"You what?!"

"Yes- it's one of the things they teach us. The hard bit was sewing up the wound until we could get evacuated out of there... Had to use clips. Bloody hurt."

"What do you do?"

"I'm... sort of... in the Navy."

This was not the time for a fuller conversation nor an examination of Izzy's other various scars, but Tegan was fascinated and determined to have a longer chat.

Not even the appetites of the village teams had managed to do too much damage to Cook's magnificent tea so there was plenty left for the two ladies.

To start with, sandwiches: egg and cress, ham and mustard, cheese and pickle, all goods produced within five miles of the Big House. Strangely, cucumber was not a favourite with the cricketers, there being an unspoken feeling that such fare was not for sportsmen, and that it gave you wind. There were fruit cakes and jam sponges and Cook's infamous Lemon Drizzle Cake which almost brought team mates to fisticuffs as it disappeared so quickly. There were scotch eggs, sausage rolls, quiches and flans, depending on when and where you were brought up and of course, scones. There was a surreptitious eye kept on the jam-first versus cream-first schisms; good old Cornish boys insisted on the jam first but there was a definite movement among the incomers that the cream was like luxurious butter and had to be there in place to take the ultimate benison of the strawberry jam. Tea was plentiful and strong.

The players abandoned all hostility when faced with such largesse and chatted and mingled together.

After that magnificent tea, Steve the farmer and Alf the milkman opened the batting for Porthwallow, for the simple reason that they both had to get back to work; Steve to milk his herd and Alf to distribute the yield of a few days previous. Sir Cosmo was in something of a quandary as to how to spread his rather limited armoury. He was pretty sure that Bobby would be good, but equally certain that he would want to wait until Tegan appeared. Similarly, he felt that Abel would want a chance to have his own back at Jake. So many personal set-tos and affrays. He wondered if the postman could bowl. After six balls, only three of them legal, he had discovered that the answer was 'no'. Two wides and a beamer, which Steve hit for six, a single, a four and enormous applause when one actually pitched on the cut strip of the wicket and within hitting distance which Alf subsequently missed, followed by three singles. Seventeen off the over. With all wickets standing. At this rate, the match would be finished by the tenth over. Cosmo decided to take his medicine early and so, as much to stop the man's importuning gaze as to benefit the team, he called up the doctor.

The doctor knew a thing or two about the theory of bowling and fielding. The problem was, he couldn't put them into practise. Forgetting that he was well over fifty, he measured out a twelve pace run up, bringing him level with Philip standing at Long Off, where he was making a daisy chain, a skill learned here in Mena Dhu in his childhood and once learned, never forgotten. It was something he and the more aesthetic of his fellow students at prep school would practise in 'E' game- the lowest of the low- while the master in charge, equally inept in sport, read the poems of Sappho, aloud, in the original Greek. Such an education can no longer be obtained anywhere these days, not even for ready money.

The doctor, hyped by the occasion and being the focus of attention, forgot all about warming up and stretching, bounded off towards the back of the umpire but had taken no more than six energetic strides when his right hamstring went- audibly! Unable to stop and in absolute agony, he hobbled on and cannoned into the unsuspecting Charlie who, as he fell, yelled 'No ball', stuck out his right arm in the designated manner and dislocated his shoulder as he landed. Not seven balls into the innings and one man and an umpire down. And one of the disabled was the designated medical officer!

"I wonder," came a voice. "can I be of any assistance?" It was Inspector Foot, tiptoeing among the fallen. "We do do First Aid, you know."

"Naw," It was Abel, the groundsman, pushing past. "'Amstring. Seen it reg'lar. Up Lord's. Only one thing for it- I.C.E. That's Ice. Compression. Elevation. Normally a packet of peas from the freezer strapped to 'is thigh but I seed Cooky with buckets of the real stuff fer the booze over there. Proper. Strap a towelful round 'im an' pour some o' the contents o' they bottles down 'is throat, 'e'll be right as rain dreckly. In about six weeks."

While some were seeing to the doctor, Izzy, Tegan and Bobby had picked up Charlie who was standing and suffering, almost in silence.

"Tegan," said Izzy. "Did you notice in my kit? Like a little wash bag? The Red one? Could you fetch it? Now. Charlie, I'm going to ask you to suffer something most of the young ladies in Porthwallow would twang their bra-straps for- I want you to let Bobby give you a big hug. Do you mind?"

The old man was in too much pain to be able to think of one of his usual rude put-downs.

"Go on, then- but no tongues!"

Bobby looked anxiously at the little woman who was so obviously in control of the situation.

Under her breath, she said: "I'm just going to pop his shoulder back in. But you need to distract him. So when I say: 'Oh, look' and point over there, I want you to make sure he looks."

It just so happened that Tegan came tripping down the caravan steps with Izzie's bag and the poetry of the motion was enough to distract any man:

"Oh, look" said Izzie, placing one hand on the old man's shoulder.

"Isn't she lovely?" Bobby's was an automatic reaction, Izzie yanked and Charlie's was:

"She certainly is tha- AAH!" A satisfactory 'pop' was heard and he gently tested his joint.

"Good as new! You should do this fer a livin', maid." Izzie was busied with her little bag, from which she withdrew a syringe and a vial.

"You're not allergic to anything, are you, sir?"

"Dun you 'sir' me no 'sir', maid. Tis Charlie and 'No', not so far as I know and tis too late to find out now,"

"Arm or bum?"

"I don't think tis proper fer you to be stickin' anything in my backside, miss, so, arm'll have to do, so long as tis not the one you just bin payin' fast and loose with!"

Izzie rolled up Charlie's left sleeve, jabbed in the morphine and gave it a good rub.

"There. Soon, you'll be feeling no pain, but probably very little else, either, so I think we're going to need a new umpire."

"Well, as I said just now," said Inspector Foot in his smarmiest voice, which he thought impressed the ladies, "Can I be of help there? The law personified and all that!" he guffawed, alone. "I can at least count to six!"

"Yeah, with 'is 'and in 'is pocket" said Hezekiah and the village team exploded.

"But we need another bowler- or fielder, at least. Do we have any offers?" Cosmo looked expectantly around the crowd but his look went unrewarded until a little voice was heard.

"Sandy can play," shouted Jake, a cry taken up by his father Michael, and Sandy, the primary school teacher who just so happened to be wearing what, with the exception of the pink sweater, unnecessary in that weather, could pass for cricket gear, stepped forward.

"But no lobs! "said Michael." It was this young lady who taught Jake about underarm."

"Under-hand, if you ask me," muttered Abel to the Salt lad, still not having got over the embarrassment of facing the little boy.

"So let battle re-commence." And, with the doctor, his leg wrapped in ice up in the air, lying on the bunk in the ladies' caravan, a bottle of champagne at hand and Charlie, leant up against the pavilion with the rum bottle aiding the morphine, the Big House team took to the field again.

Abel explained that as soon as the doctor had hit the umpire, the ball was dead, so they could start the second over again, almost half an hour after the end of the first.

"I ain't got time ter 'ang about," said Steve, "My ladies'll be bustin'." As with any little difficulty in Life, Sir Cosmo turned to his butler, Hives, for extrication and threw him the ball.

"Let's have a couple of overs of the old stuff."

Hives did at least have a stretch to avoid pulling anything but his first delivery ended up in the chaos of the tea table, narrowly missing the Cook. His second, however, the farmer dollied gently into the hands of Aleksy whose cry of: "Is this it?" was near enough to the traditional appeal for Inspector Foot to agree to raise a finger magisterially. He enjoyed the outcome, a rush of power rarely experienced in his day job.

This brought Michael to the wicket, accompanied, inevitably, by the screams of ladies both young and not so young. To see the leader of one of the world's more successful rock bands in the flesh, and up close as well, caused one or two of them to appear to faint but those with them who had come simply for the cricket ignored them and like unsuccessful 'diving' international footballers, they recovered remarkably quickly.

Michael could play, and not just the guitar. His stance was precise and no-one who knows the game would have been surprised to learn that the MCC Coaching Manual had been among his recent bedside reading. Even Sandy dipped into it.

The left elbow was correctly erect, the feet slightly apart and he favoured the older technique of the bat touching the ground, rather than the Graham Gooch-style raised bat, as at baseball.

His bat came down perpendicularly, the ball shot through the gully and he called to Alf to run, which he did. Cosmo and Jago heaved sighs of relief. At least they might make a game of it.

As with just about everything in Life, Hives disported himself rather well. With his height, he had once been quite a handful, and even now, nearing his seventh decade, he still had the guile of a fox and the action of a thoroughbred. Alf thrashed about for a while, connecting occasionally but there were no quick singles and soon, catching his wife's eye as she ostentatiously tapped her wrist, he missed a straight one and went off to work.

Which brought in Hezekiah Pemberthy. A true Cornishman, H. was not very tall but as wide as a door, and strong with it. Years of hefting breeze blocks and hauling crab pots meant that if he hit a ball, it remained hit. The problem was seeing it. H. was not a prepossessing man; in fact, he was positively ugly, but he was reluctant to wear his glasses.

"Mek me look like a cross between that Groucho Marx and fuckin' John Lennon."

So, without his glasses, he had a variety of targets to try to focus on; laws of averages meant that he chose the right one at least twice an over and he and Michael pushed the score on well. However, it was not long before his luck ran out; he selected one of the missiles that wasn't there and he edged a ball from Hives into his master's awaiting gloves.

Another anticipatory cheer went up when it was seen that Tegan was next man in.

Hives was nothing if not a gentleman and his first ball to Tegan, the last of his spell, was a gentle long hop outside the off stump which she played through the covers for a single. This meant that she was facing the new bowler. Who, of course, was Bobby.

Bobby was a nice man, a good man, a gentleman. He

had played against some very capable cricketers in his short career but he had never been faced with his present quandary, namely how to bowl against the woman he loved. True, she had bamboozled him but there was a tendency for this in most of their relationship, anyway. But he rarely surprised her. He could of course send one down at eighty miles an hour and possibly clean bowl her but equally possibly hurt her, and that he would never do. He had to use guile.

The first two were at a medium pace, outside the off stump; if she was to get out to those, it would be her own fault. In fact, she played both easily and ran two off both. Michel was more than happy to stand at the other end, watch and do as he was told. The next was a little quicker and a little straighter and she had to pay it the respect it was due. Straight bat for nought. The next, squeezed down to Third Man for a single. Bobby had none of the reservations about bowling properly to Michael and the final two balls of Bobby's over had him dancing as he rarely did at one of his own concerts.

The next over, bowled by the boy Salt, produced four singles and so it was Bobby versus Tegan again. An old ploy- the first ball was off the longer run and quite fast, but Tegan hit it for four, a smile on her lips; the second, the same length run but half the speed of delivery and an off cutter to boot. Tegan was majestic in the pose she held, even after she heard the clatter of the bails.

"Bastard!" she said, sweetly and kissed Bobby as she walked off.

Nathan did not last long as he was more bemused by being the company of a rock star than by the bowling of Bobby, who bowled a similar cutter with a similar effect.

There was a hum of conversation by the scoreboard, from which a treble voice could be heard: "Oh, please, Mr Jago" with the gentle voices of the Vicar and Jeremy supporting the plea.

And so the diminutive figure of Jake, pads up to his waist, waddled out. His gait was restricted even further by the fact that he had insisted on stuffing a box down his pants and even the most modest protector looked like some sort of abdominal growth on the poor boy.

But he was to bat with his father!

"And remember, run up and down. No haring off to first base."

Bobby Hawkins' good nature has been stressed elsewhere and it was simply not in him to bowl even moderately fast at the boy. However, he was not used to bowling slowly and his first came down at about the same speed as a Little league softball pitch, something that Jake was well used to, and while he has not strong enough to reach the boundary, he leathered the thing and hard towards, and past his father.

"That's ma boy!" called Michael, in his much-loved parody of *Spike* from 'Tom and Jerry'. But he had to come back to reality to stop his son rushing back again, leaving both out their ground.

"No! Wait! NO!"

Bobby had no qualms about bowling at Michael, which he did, comprehensively. 65 for 6. Since the forces of this world were tottering, Jago decided to call upon those of the next.

"Vicar? Cometh the hour an' all that? That's the Bible, innit?"

"Actually, no- perhaps- um 'Christ the Royal master, leads against the foe', might be more apposite but, Jago, I should be more than happy to go in but I really must insist that Jeremy precedes me in this. I know my place in this pecking order."

"Trevor?" and a slight shrug was all the opposition that Jeremy made to his partner's suggestion before he took a faded old cap of black, red and yellow from his bag and walked out.

Abel Tonkin was the only one present, certainly among those playing, who recognised the I-Zingari colours.

His bat was wood- just wood. Brown wood. None of the synthetic coverings and garish logos of the current bludgeons, and about half the size but it was like a wand in his hands.

Abel had entered the fray, determined to put the little squirt in his place with some real spin bowling.

While he had been at Lord's, his hero had been Phil Edmonds. Philippe-Henri Edmonds, the Middlesex and England star who smote mightily, right-handed, down the order and bowled classic slow left-arm spin. He was also something of a throwback, a gentleman in the world of sweaty professionals, although with a temper that belied his balding, aristocratic appearance. While Abel could do nothing about his breeding or his hairline, he could at least copy the bowling action and attempt the same effect.

Jake knew nothing about any of this and flat-batted his first ball towards the cover boundary, yelling to Jeremy to: "C'mon- Move your butt!". They ran three but a cry of "Jake!" was heard from the boundary above the applause and Jake realised that his father disapproved.

"Any more of that and I'll retire you, hurt!"

"Sorry, sir."

Jeremy was unperturbed. He stroked the rest of Abel's over around the ground, with Jago moving a fieldsman to where the previous ball had gone and where the next would not. Eight off the over.

"Well, my dear" said Cosmo without thinking to Izzy, who happened to find herself in the slips, next to him, "To misquote Frank Sinatra: It has to be you."

"I'm very sorry, my Lord, "she said, bashfully, "But I can't. Not any more. I fell off a Somali pirate."

"Man?"

"Ship. I still have the scars. I can show you sometime and somewhere less public-"

Cosmo was all for cancelling the match then and there.

"But I can't really lift my right arm much above shoulder height. Which rather hampers the cliff climbing. I was doing that kayaking to help recuperate. Under arm, yes, but I think we've done that one to death."

"So we have a choice, Aleksy, Philip or the long arm of the law."

"Or you?"

"No- I always think that smacks of *amour-propre* when the keeper takes off his pads and bowls, don't you? Doesn't say much about the rest of his team."

"Save Aleksy for his oppo, if needs be. I do think you should give Cousin Philip a go. He didn't bat long."

"Ah, but he has visited the garage- seen the family collection of cars. We've got a Panhard, a very early Renauld, an E type- for a while, my father took to buying a Rolls each year, but we ran out of stabling and realised they weren't much of an investment, so sold all but the best. It seems they're like wine- some years better than the other. Anyway, Philip was in his element and his visit was worth it just for that. Philip?"

He called to his cousin who was now wearing his daisy chain and turning over gently at Mid Off.

"Vrumm."

"Fancy a bowl?"

"Oh, I say, Well, there's that rather nice Chinese eggshell one you've got in the hallway..."

"No, no- cricket. Bowl the ball."

"Oh, my! Bit of extra choke called for here. Vrumm! Of course. A de Coverlet never says no! At least, not often."

He walked to the wicket where Inspector Foot stood.

"You're the fuzz? Is that right?" and marched past before the man could speak.

"And who are we bowling to? Not that dear little boy?" And he wiped his glasses with the silk handkerchief that he had in his pocket and proceeded to put them away carefully.

Foot turned to look. "Ready? "

Philip nodded and Foot had hardly the time to say: "Play" before Philip bundled him aside and bowled quite an acceptable ball. Jake played it carefully back.

"Again?" Philip asked of his cousin.

"Please."

And again, a very acceptable military medium trundled down the track.

"Enough?"

"No, you're doing fine. Maybe a tad faster?"

"Ahah", and he mimed a racing gear change and his vroom-vrooms became a tone higher.

This time Jake hit it and called "Run".

"Jolly good shot," said Philip, without a trace of sarcasm.

Jeremy squared up, ready to face, when Philip, looking up, said: "Oh, I say, I do like your cap. Bringing a bit of colour into this otherwise bleached and blanched world. Jolly good show."

They played the final two balls for two runs apiece- honours just about equal. And Abel had the boy in his sights again.

Although Abel rarely talked about his time on the Ground Staff at Lord's, he was justifiably proud of his achievements. He would have liked a more prestigious ground to care for, but the de Coverlets did pay extremely well, and provide a cottage in the estate. So for a man of his experience and self-esteem, to be hit all over the ground by a mere child and a quasi-yank at that, dented his pride.

He trotted in on his tiptoes, as his idol had done and gave the ball a prodigious snap; but Jake was used to playing against Sandy's underarm spinners in the garden and so he watched it carefully and pulled it through midwicket to the boundary.

That was it!

Abel hadn't tried to bowl a 'chinaman'- the left armer's reverse spinner- for years but now was the hour. He contorted everything, including his face to make the ball spin, which it did and clean bowled the boy.

"Hey, not fair. I mean, sure, neat ball but that man was making faces- is that allowed?"

"I 'm afraid so," said Jeremy. "There's nothing we can do about the gifts God gives us."

"Well, I just hope the wind changes and he stays that way." And he marched off to considerable applause.

Which brought the Vicar to the crease and just as Jago had imagined in the pub weeks ago, the two of them at eight and nine held on.

Until the end of the penultimate over when the Vicar, with visions of glory, humming: 'Lo he comes in clouds descending', wafted, head in air, and was bowled. Which brought Felicks to the wicket, the score spelled out on the old board in tin numbers, no high-tech here.

"Aleksy," said Cosmo.

"My lord?"

"Would you like to bowl?"

"To my friend?"

"Yes."

"Yes, plizz, my lord."

Abel had taught the Poles the basics of the game; Aleksy's no longer contorted himself like someone attempting an impression of Quasimodo when he bowled and Felicks no longer swung as if his bat were an axe, his more accustomed blade. Aleksys' action was still awkward and Felicks' stance more like that of an off-duty headsman but neither the ball nor the stroke was the worst seen that afternoon by a long way. Felicks managed to reach the second and to hit it, so Jeremy called him through for two. The cry of triumph that issued forth from Felicks' throat would have been recognised and feared thousands of years ago by Roman legionaries facing the Germani in the depths of the Black Forest. Heartily felt. The next ball was not so well hit, so Jeremy called for one and, being the sort of person he was, felt that it was only right to miss the next, to allow his captain the kudos of either saving or winning the game.

"Bugger me!" said Jago, quickly buckling on his pads and searching frantically for a box. "I thought they was going to do it."

"You'll have to hurry up there, or I shall have to time you out." Inspector Foot's supposed little joke fell flatter than Constable Drake's feet.

"You do that and I 'sll shove your teeth so far down your throat, you'll 'ave to brush they up yer arse, mate." said Jago as he bustled to the wicket.

"Right arm over, two to come." And four to win.

"You ready, boy?" called Jago to the Pole.

"Abso-bloody-lootly, my lord."

He hit it, no matter where and they ran one.

Jago to face the last ball. He hit it along the ground- at least he wasn't going to be caught and he raced down the wicket-

"Just keep running!"

Sadly, the subtlety was lost in translation; or rather he did exactly as ordered. He ran. Straight up the wicket and off the field of play straight to the pavilion, where uproar reigned. Only one run!

They had lost by one run!

There was bitter tears and false humility all round, the Big House players clapping each other on the various backs and scowls galore among the villagers when a voice was heard: "Hey, dad, when the scores are the same, ain't that what they call a 'tie'?"

"Isn't that." It was Sandy, helping with Jake's 'anglification'. "Why?"

"We both got the same amount."

"No, son. Check the score book."

"No, you check the score books, dad. I counted. In my head- Mister Cosmo, he got twenty an' then Bobby, he got thirty-six..." And gradually he reeled off both teams' individual scores. Extras included. Henry Lake, the shop-keeping umpire, deemed to be the most obvious accountant among them, checked his figures on the calculator app on his phone...

"He's right. The boy is absolutely right. The scorers missed the one that he scored off Mr Philip de Coverlet."

"Super shot, that," said Philip, as if to underline the truth.

"And you don't question Jake's sums," said Sandy. "In his head, he's as quick as a calculator."

"So, we didn't lose after all?"

"No," said his very proud father. "Thanks to you."

Chapter 15

In the pub, things were getting mellow. Jake had fallen to sleep on a bench and Sandy was leaning close against Michael. Jago had his arms on the table and was sighing. It was at times like these that he remembered Nicole. H. had been good and gone home to his wife but Bobby, once he had reinstated his grandfather, had come back down to fraternise. Even Trevor and Jeremy had stayed on, sipping ginger wine.

Jago had to ask.

"Jeremy, how come... well, you'm obviously so good. Why d'you stop playing?"

"The other players."

"Surely nobody makes a thing about..." He wasn't sure what term they accepted so twiddled his fingers...

"Being gay? No, it's not that, though there are still very few of us who will admit it. No, it's because they're so boring. All they ever talk about it cricket. After the game, you'd go to the pub, they'd sit in front of gallons of lager- this was before all these new diets they have now- and talk about the game, analyse it, the shots they'd played, ball by ball almost, then talk about other cricketers, the England team, whatever, as long as it was cricket. Cricket, cricket! I gave up the idea of being a professional for fear of early brain death."

"Well, I think he's a very lucky man." Tegan expressed her views to the almost-empty bar of *The de Coverlet Arms.*

"Unsung King of England who's worth billions?" said Bobby. "I probably agree with you."

"No, I mean, finding Izzie."

"Well, I rather think she found him. Seems she'd had a crush on him for years. Ever since she met him at Gramp's birthday party." Here he grew silent but could not restrain himself for long.

"Um... I don't suppose this has given you any... ideas?"

"No. Nothing definite," And she popped a kiss on his lips. "But it has set me thinking."

The Cricket Match being out of the way and such a surprising success, following on from last year's Happening, inevitably the Brains' Trust that met irregularly in the bar of the pub was faced by the question: what next?

Something was alive in the old village; it was not possible to put one's finger on it but it was definitely something.

The Vicar had noticed it.

"In the past," he said, "it really was just the oldies cramming for their finals but even some of the young families have started to come to church..."

"'Tis down to Michael."

"Oh, come now," said Michael, his usual modesty to the fore. The transformation from the front man of one of the most successful stadia rock bands in the world to this gentle and slightly balding *pater familias* in his pristine fisherman's smock, tailored jeans and yellow wellies was remarkable. His voice rarely raised above a murmur, as long as he was being agreed with; when not, there could be a hardness that would countenance no opposition and hinted at the steel within.

"But it's true," said Jeremy, the Vicar's partner. "You only have to watch them. I mean, Trevor's busy but I can look out at those faces, and far more of them are in the direction of Michael's seat as Choir Master than Trevor's."

"Can hardly blame them," said the Vicar, grudgingly.

"Well, enough said," said Michael and they knew to go on. "What would normally happen this time of year?!"

Jeremy consulted the Church diary.

"Well, it would have been the Church Fete-"

"Hah!" cried H., "The fete worse n' death!"

"Thank you, H,"

"No, but tis true," said the builder. "Backalong weren't too bad. But recently, no reflection on your worship, but it really was a case of' two or three gathered together in thy name- you an' Jezzer, and you wasn't always sure of the third!"

"How come you quote the Bible like that an' never come to Church?"

"I 'ad enough of it when I was a tacker. Services twice on Sundays AND Sunday afternoon Sunday School. All us kids was sent along, strict as strict. Twas only later we realised that Sunday afternoons was the only time our parents could guarantee a bit of time for themselves and their weekly shag!"

"Thank you, H, for that little bit of social history!" said Tegan behind the bar.

"But tis true. Don't need it now cos they got their phones and I-pads and that. Parents could be swinging naked from the light shades and the kids wouldn't notice."

"And Harvest Festival." said Michael. "I remember in the Cathedral." Michael had been a chorister at Bristol Cathedral. "We should have a Harvest Festival."

"Your enthusiasm is admirable," said Trevor, "But the last time we had one, the entire contribution from the congregation was two tins of beans, a packet of Smash, a pair of coconuts and a handful of daffodils stolen from the Vicarage garden. We saw them!"

"I had to hurry into Morrison's to buy something to make it even vaguely acceptable," said Jeremy.

"And even then," said Jago, remembering, "the whole coconuts seemed rather out of place, seeing as they had been left over from the shy stall at the Fete. Not many fresh coconuts harvested round here."

"And there was a rather unfortunate story attached to that, as well. Have you met Sidney Dunn? Lives out in the country but was church warden and verger for a while- a rather short while. He undertook to look after the coconut shy and there were great cries of skull-duggery and malfeasance from that corner of the church yard- we held the Fete there because we knew that not many would come- but it seems some of the cricketers from St Austell had come especially to show off their prowess to their lady friends and no matter how many times they had hit a nut, nothing happened. It appeared that Sidney had superglued them to the cups. We were forced to return their money and insist that Sid retire. It wasn't too bad- we rarely have call for a verger these days. There is what I call the Brazen brigade- the old- no, they don't like being called 'old'- a 'not so young' team of the ladies who congregate at the cafe most mornings for white coffee and filthy gossip- they've taken over the cleaning of the church. I think they're hoping for extra brownie points when they come up against St Peter at the Pearly gates- you know, several years dusting the Vestry to counterbalance their behaviour with the Yanks that weekend before Invasion."

With Sir Cosmo's marriage beyond their sphere of influence and as it had been the men who had planned the cricket match, the ladies felt it was they who should work on the next keystone of Porthwallow's social year, the church Fete and Harvest Festival.

"Fete AND Harvest festival!?" exclaimed Janice. "Never 'eard of anything like it in me life!"

"Don't be ridiklus," replied Maggie, a regular repost to a regular exclamation. "Tweren't that far backalong when us 'ad they two together, regular. I remember when I was a little girl..." An event that happened so often that no-one listened any more for any special revelation.

"If it's all gonna be rock an' roll, then I for one shall not be going."

"Don't be ridiklus. 'Oo said it was anything to do with rock an' roll. And you liked it when that Michael brung 'is band in on the landing craft."

"I never said I liked it."

"No-one heard you complain. And I saw you dancin' on the quay with the rest of us."

"Would you ...?" This was Jenny, rather young to be a regular member of the circle but who was on waitress duty and always guaranteed to spice things up a bit, especially on what seen to be her specialist subject.

"You know... with Michael?"

"Whatjamean?... Nookie an' that!?"

Well, that was the start of a conversation about animal magnetism that called for a fresh round of coffees, for each in her own way had something to add but it was stopped in its tracks when Binnie Long said: "I had a donkey once."

Now, the phrases used to describe Binnie Long varied with those who invented them.

'One sandwich short of a picnic' was one of the kinder.

'Not one of our more precocious brethren', was another, offer by an arrogant cow who should have known better.

'Not the sharpest needle in the haystack,' was another which displayed the confusion of the insulter just as much as of the insultee.

None of them was sure whether Binnie was joining in the conversation about sexual relations or starting off on her own special tangent.

"Wot?" It was Maggie who broke the silence.

"My father-" began Binnie and some of the others were dreading what awful revelations were about to be released. She started again- "My father- God rest 'is soul- "And the pent-up breaths were released.

"'E used to keep donkeys-"

"'E did 'n all." said Betty. "I remember- kept 'em in the top field-"

"Ere" said Binnie, "'oo's story is it? My father used to keep donkeys. Fer deliverin' coal an' that round the village. Half they new houses 'ad all their timber and wot's that stuff fer stickin' stuff together?" Somebody offered "Superglue," but they were obviously not on Binnie's wavelength. "Naw! Cement, that's it- cement. An' I 'ad a special favourite as I looked after. I called 'en 'Methusalah' after matey in the Bible. The old one. Cos 'ee was old. The donk. That is. Anyway, us used to ride they on the sand at 'Church Fete. Backalong. O'course but I was thinkin'-"

"Brilliant, dear," said Bunty, "Donkey rides. If the tide's right. But we don't have donkeys any more- they use dumper trucks. And quad bikes."

"We could race quad bikes?!" offered an enthusiast but she was rightly ignored."

"Naw but they 'as 'em down Looe- well, 'tother side- a Donkey Sanctuary. We could ask. All my father's went there when he passed."

"No, no!" offered one of the ladies who had taken part. "Mobility scooters! Like at the Regatta."

Mena Dhu

To begin with, the men in the pub were reluctant to combine with the women from the tearooms. As always, both sides felt that they could do perfectly well without the other and it was voiced over the skinny lattes that, come universal IVF, it would be easy to prove, but the Vicar, being non-aligned and Michael, his relationship with the young school mistress being very discrete, managed to charm the ladies, while Tegan, a foot in each camp, and Bobby, who did whatever Tegan wanted, soon managed to establish some sort of working relationship. While not as acerbic as some of the recent discussions in Europe, there were times when Jeremy, the secretary to the committee, longed to emulate his long-dead predecessor, Leonid Kruschev at the United Nations, and bang the table with his shoe in frustration.

It was the ladies' predilection to talk that was the cause of this dissatisfaction. Even when he produced agendas, beautifully printed on his Apple Mac, Jeremy was not able to stop them talking and, as was so often the case with them, one thing led to another and it was nine o'clock, the *terminus ad quem* agreed by all, before they got half way through.

Eventually, H. put his foot down. Consciously curbing his appetite for profanity, he said: "Look, either we'm 'ere to 'elp the Vicar with 'is fete worse'n death or we'm 'ere to gab, an' if that's the case, I resign."

"Oh," said Bunty, "That's rather abrupt!"

"Abrupt, my ar-" and then he remembered himself, "My aunt Fanny!"

But with Jeremy Simmonds' gentle dexterity, they produced an agreement which they all admitted was to be ideal.

The fact that Cosmo de Coverlet, prompted by Izzy, had offered the lawn in front of the House for the Fete greatly improved matters. And when Cook promised to provide refreshments but not to enter any of her jams or chutneys into the competition- "'Er's nigh on perfessional!" had been the opinion emanating from *The Copper Kettle*- and his Lordship had offered to top up the usual prizes of a £5 voucher from ASDA, people got to looking out the old cups that had been contested and polishing them up again.

Of course, the Harvest Festival had taken place in St Wallow, the lovely old church out in the woods above the village. Compared to the last celebration of the rather pagan festivities that had been invented by another Cornish vicar, the Reverend Robert Hawker, back in the middle of the nineteenth century in an attempt to fill his often empty church at Morwenstow- he was often only accompanied at his morning services by the dogs and cats of the church town farm, plus a pet pig-this one was magnificent. Instead of the previous display of two tins of beans and the packet of Smash, the family from the farm had started things off by arranging stooks of hay in the old-fashioned way to stand below the pulpit. Rather than rolling it all in bales clad in black plastic, these looked like golden fountains.

Apples had always been plentiful- proof of which being the

excellent local cider- and Sandy from the school had arranged some scrumping expeditions which were verging on the illegal, but which provided an excellent display at the altar rail. Flowers filled every window sill so that when the sun shone through the ancient stained glass, it was as if the blooms had been sprayed by a rainbow. While Cornish palm trees are not quite the same as those on tropical islands, they can have impressive branches and one of the lady gardeners was persuaded to trim a few of hers to add a triumphal arch over the doorway. Trevor did think of saying that they might be confusing Harvest Festival with Palm Sunday but decided against it.

While they didn't feature in such services upcountry, fresh fish- indeed, some fresh pilchards, something of a rarity- appeared on the morning of the service. Jago and H. had been out first thing and thought that there must be something in this religion thing because they hit a small shoal and had a very fair display. No-one was surprised that these rarities disappeared with the elder members of the congregation after the service.

And Michael agreed to sing.

He had none of the Angels with him this time. And the fact that he would sing at all was kept something of a secret as they didn't want too many fans coming from far and wide. And he was nervous.

"I haven't felt like this," he told Jake and Sandy, sitting in the choir stalls as the body of the church filled, some of them being first-time attendees, swept along by the local enthusiasm. Cosmo, Izzy, Hives and Mrs Walker slipped into the back row where Bobby sat with Tegan and the Admiral.

"Not since back in the Cathedral when I sang 'Away in a manger' at Christmas. I was ten."

"Wow, that must have been, like, in the Stone Age!" said Jake.

"Enough of that."

But when he started the opening bars of "We Plough the fields and scatter," there was something of a wobble in his voice but soon the professional took over and his magnificent baritone filled the old place and when, looking round at Sandy and Jake, he finished the final refrain: "Then thank the Lord, oh, thank the Lord, For all His love," the congregation, unused to the niceties of church services, burst into applause.

Chapter 16

And then on to the Fete up at the Big House.

To begin with, the old ladies said they wouldn't go.

"'Tis all very well, 'im bein' a lord an' that but tis we old folk as 'as to walk up that 'ill and me with my legs. Well, I just in't goin', 'tis as simple as that." But these complaints were quashed when it was learned that Sir Cosmo had agreed to let the old Bedford SB5 bus out of his incalculably valuable collection of motor vehicles, to be used to ferry the villagers back and forth. Inevitably, Philip was fussing around, ensuring that everything was working perfectly, but he was not allowed to drive it on public roads, having temporarily lost his license whilst being an Austin Healey Frogeye Sprite in Penge.

The visitors were dropped off in front of the house and subtly diverted away from the front door to the lawn where all the stalls were set up. This strategic task Cosmo had allotted to himself so most people thought he must be a member of staff, which was rather the effect he was after. It was Philip who, elated by the appearance of the old bus, wandered through the crowd as if he owned the place. His wardrobe of the same flannels which he had sported for the cricket match, his Cambridge college blazer, panama hat and a turquoise silk scarf at his throat made him appear quite the Lord of the

Manor. Indeed, some of the elder locals touched where their forelocks would have been had they not been Brylcreem'd back for the occasion.

Those who were to take part in the mobility scooter races had had their steeds delivered for them; the thought of driving them all the way up from the village was a daunting one and none of them was really sure that their battery would last that far. And anyway, they did not want to forgo the chance of riding on the old bus. The memories that the sight, smell and feel on the posterior had generated were legion and they were all talking at once. Fortunately, the races were not on for a while and the rest of the crowd had a chance to spend money at all the traditional stalls.

At the White Elephant stall, quite a few youngsters asked after the whereabouts of said pachyderm but even when the origin of the phrase was explained, as referring to unwanted albinos in Thailand, they seemed little wiser.

'Sticking the Tail on the Donkey' was much more self-explanatory and much simple hilarity was still to be had in this hi-tech age, especially when the attempts of the blind-folded contestants zoned in on the neddy's genitals.

Trevor himself ruled over the coconut shy to ensure that, this year, there was no doubt about the free-range disposition of the nuts. It did help having Jeremy at his side; not everyone had heard of his expertise exhibited in the Cricket match, so when people- usually teenaged youths- complained that 'they nuts is stuck on', Jeremy would apparently aimlessly pick up one of the wooden balls and send it pinging its way as if to the top of the stumps, thereby inevitably dislodging the prize. This would leave the plaintiff speechless and red-faced in front of his admirers. Jeremy would then add insult to injury by offering the nut to the accuser.

The Lucky Dip was ruled by Jago; as a carpenter, he had a near endless supply of sawdust and in a barrel full of the stuff, he had hidden a range of prizes, all exquisitely wrapped, so little fingers could not guess at their contents by fumbling them first. Some were simply sweets but , rather like a proper Christmas pudding with at least one high denomination coin hidden within, there were a couple of special packages, hiding silver Cornish flags. Once one had been revealed, the flow of punters to the stall increased vastly.

The greatest hilarity came from within a little tent with a sign 'Madame Hortense- fortune teller' above 'Crystal balls' over the entrance. At the door sat Nathan, a pirate's scarf tied round his head. It was he who took the money and warned against supernatural uprisings. Inside, though nobody ever said, sat Hezekiah, behind a table on which stood a crystal ball. He too had a scarf tied round his head, but this scarf had little cymbals attached which tinkled whenever he moved. He wore a diaphanous blouse, a silver waistcoat and, though they were never seen, harem pants. His wife, Bev, had spent an uproarious half-hour making him up and they promised each other that they'd do it again, one night when they had nothing else on!

With all the women, and his clientele was mainly female, he would start: "I see a tall dark stranger who you will meet very soon" and considering Nathan on the door was well over six-foot and bronzed with working outdoors, H. was invariably right.

If his tentative: "I can see children," was met with: "But I'm not even married yet," his comeback was "Well, what are doing tonight?"; if the customer was obviously a parent, he would say: "Bad news. You could be losing a bit of money."

If the subject asked: "When?", he would reply: "This afternoon- get your hand in your pocket, you tight git."

One middle-aged visitor to the area who had heard that the event was to be held in the Mena Dhu grounds and was eager to take this rare opportunity, went up to Philip, whom she supposed to be in charge and said: "That... person in the tent is a charlatan!"

But Philip simply replied: "Absolutely. And it's so good of him to give up his only spare afternoon this month from his job as top brain surgeon at Great Ormond Street Children's Hospital to come all this way down and help. And he paid his own expenses."

The woman dropped a twenty-pound note into one of the collecting buckets and fled.

Steve, from the farm, had brought along several late young lambs and was not amused by H.'s cry of "Lunch!"

Along with the lambs, he had brought his two little daughters, both of whom kept rabbits. Although they were eventually intended for the pot, the buns made a welcome addition to the Animal Magic Corner. The farmyard bitch had just whelped as well and so there were several darling bundles for the children to hold, although the father was kept at home, for fear of him making any further attempts at procreation on unsuspecting visitors. Or at least on their dogs.

Young chicks were always popular, little yellow feather bundles, and Steve had made a special effort and brought one of the piglets which spent most the afternoon ploughing up Abel's front lawn with its snout.

Jennie and two of the surviving members of the now-defunct Theatre Club had set up a Face Painting stall which proved very popular with the children. They could either be a monster or an animal of their choice- within reason- one child requested to be made up as a stegosaurus. When that request was refused, he asked to be a komodo dragon, but Jennie explained that they did not a suitable flesh-colour and that he would have to either a pussycat or a doggie.

"Ok- I wanna be a bearded collie." And he sat there while they stuck a beard- a residue from one of their more ambitious productions, 'Coriolanus'- all over his face. Most made do with cats, with the exception of one little boy who wanted to be Spiderman. Jennie could not resist this challenge and spent the next half hour reproducing the picture she found on her phone.

Apple bobbing was wet, messy fun as was the more modern take on the coconut shy, namely squirting table tennis balls off candle sticks with vast water pistols. When some little boys started to be over-enthusiastic with the water pistols, H., who was on a break, grabbed both the child and the pistol and said: "Oi, stop that or else I'll stick this pistol up yer arse and pull the trigger. An enema you'll never ferget!"

Cyril Oliphant had a problem; he had not been banned specifically, of course, but had sneaked in with the local crowd and was uncertain of his target. There were apparently two de Coverlets. As he was about to try to clarify the situation, he noticed that he had been espied by Jago and Michael, both of whom had been party to him being expelled from a village hall meeting and receiving a not-so-fresh gurnard down his trousers for his meddling, while the inhabitants of the Big House knew him from the Ball. He beat a retreat to the liberationists' van, parked well out of sight for fear of the reaction its appearances might cause and left it to his trusty lieutenants.

Philip was jumping up and down, clapping his hands like a delighted child at the prospect of the races, when there was a tap on his shoulder.

"Yow De Coverlet?"

"Yes?"

"Come this way, please."

Then a voice was heard: 'And here they come!' and over the tannoy the Skaters' Waltz' could be heard as the procession of several mobility scooters appeared from the Mews, especially converted into pits for the afternoon. Mr Collard who had headed up the display during the regatta was sadly in an old-people's home, never again to take to his doughty steed. So the Admiral led them. He had proposed a racing start like that at Le Mans, where the drivers sprint across the track and leap into their cars before driving off. However, Izzy pointed out that the very nature of the vehicles and drivers rather precluded this and so he and Izzy had worked out a very complicated seeding and handicapping system, calculating what sort of start should be allowed for age, gender, general health and any advanced signs of Alzheimer's but in the end, they all raced against each other in what they refused to describe as a 'knock-out' system in case it was mistaken by any of the more enthusiastic of the contestants. The admiral would have won easily, had he not been such a gentleman, so in the end the winner was Maggie Tregenza and it was all that she could do to maintain her facade of insouciance and not smile as she was presented the inaugural Hawkins Cup for Mobility Scooter racing.

Chapter Seventeen

After Philip had been accosted by Auroch and Gaia, he followed them obediently. He had an indefinite feeling that here, back on home ground, at Mena Dhu, he, as a de Coverlet, was duty bound to do whatever was asked of him without question. When they reached the van, his feeling of laudable *'noblesse oblige'* changed to one of absolute rapture.

"Oh, I say! A Morris J-type van, circa 1958? Oh, my. Are we actually going to ride in this? Wonderful!"

Which meant that they did not have to use the chloroform that Cyril had had so much trouble acquiring. Philip was so busy admiring everything about the old van that he was unaware of where they were going, so that when they arrived back at the homestead, he could have been anywhere and not have minded. For as he got down from the J-type, he saw, dotted about the yard, bits of cars that he had not seen for years which filled him with delight.

"Could I have a tinker?"

"It's out the back," said Auroch, who had misheard him.

"Not the lavvy, daft. No, my lord, please do. Feel free to... tinker."

No-one noticed his immediate absence because, over the hilarity of the final race and presentation of the trophy, as if it had been laid on as a special extra attraction, there came the call: Fire!

Looking round, no-one could see an obvious source of fire from the lawn but it had been the boy, Salt, slipping back to his room to change into something that might impress the young ladies more than his work clothes who had seen the smoke, coming from a window in the West wing.

Immediately he pressed the button that activated the up-to-date fire alarm which, in its turn, triggered the sprinkler system in that wing. Mena Dhu may well be ancient but the de Coverlets, down the ages, had seen enough of fire to spend whatever was necessary in order to eliminate it.

The lad met Cosmo and Hives running back at the head of a motley crew and they were all greeted by the unlikely vision of old Lord de Coverlet, apparently running out of the fire towards them.

"It's Dad!" cried Cosmo

"A miracle!" said the Vicar but in fact it was the two nurses, a drip in one hand and the other arm around their care, like a nightmare rugby front row, hurrying as best they could.

"I think it's only the West wing," said one as they laid the old man down on one of Abel's handcarts. Jago, H. and Nathan, being the core of the Porthwallow volunteer fire crew, were in a quandary: if they raced back the miles to fetch their engine, more damage would be done in the ensuing time. If only they could do something now. It was Cosmo who came up with the answer.

"We've got a fire engine!" he said. And indeed, so they did.

Dating from a time before the village had had one, the Big House had had its own. Used more often for watering the tennis courts and the cricket square than any conflagration, the old AEC machine sat among the collection of priceless cars in the stables like a trusty servant among the nobs. Of course, with Philip's enthusiasm and expertise- he would always service it and give it the once-over when he visited- secretly, it was his favourite, above even the Hispano Suiza which he claimed to prefer when asked- it started immediately and there was a brief *contre-temps* as to who should be allowed to ring the bell as it was driven out of the stable towards the Big House.

By the time the county brigade arrived, the fire was out.

"But we have to be sure," said the disappointed fire captain and so they drenched the entire West wing from garret to cellar.

"And don't nobody be allowed inside till I gives the all-clear!"

"Your name isn't Foot, by any chance, is it?" asked a rather miffed Sir Cosmo.

A chastened few, Cosmo, Hives, Izzy and Mrs Walker, had gathered in the small sitting room of the Big House, while the volunteer firefighters, having dutifully washed down the Mena Dhu fire tender, were washing down several pints of their chosen tipple, courtesy of Sir Cosmo, in the pub.

"Keep a tab for me, will you, Charlie?" He had remembered to ask the old landlord, his shoulder now comfortable in a sling. "Let them have what they want, within reason."

"Don't worry, my Lord," said Trevor, the Vicar, "I'll keep a watchful eye over my flock. And if there's anything we can do to help- we're quite good at Garden Party fund raisers..."

Cosmo simply smiled; funds were no problem- it was purely the bother of having to clean up. His father was installed in one of the guest rooms and the nurses assured his son that he had obviously enjoyed his day out. In fact, one said that she definitely heard him say something, which she maintained had been: "More!"

It was when the fire officer came to report that things became complicated.

"Everything all right now, is it Officer? "asked Sir Cosmo, pressing a £50 note into the man's hand. "For the Firemen's Ball, or whatever you have these days?"

"That's very kind of you, sir but the trouble is... what we found."

"What!?" Cosmo was worried that the water might have seeped as far as his study and the Playboy collection.

"Well, sir. To put it bluntly- the corpses."

"Corpses!?"

"Sorry, that's me really rather overstating the case. Perhaps I should really say 'corpse'. Singular."

It was then that they noticed the plastic evidence bag with

a dead rat in it.

"If that's your corpse, officer..." began Hives before the other stopped him.

"Sorry, Mr Hives- That was me being melodramatic. This here is what we in Fire Investigation call 'evidence'."

"Can I see that? "asked Izzie, unexpectedly snatching at the rat.

"The other is, well, was a person. Should any of you involved in this incident require counselling, we do have forms. Or a website. Or we're on Facebook. Or Twitter."

"Thank you very much but we don't even know who's involved. Where did you find it?"

"It is a corpse of an elderly female. In the last room on the top floor. I have to apologise- we axed it, thinking... well, not really thinking. But the door was unlocked."

"That's Nanny Thomlinson's old room."

And so it proved. And the body was of Nanny Thomlinson, too.

"But she left years ago," said Mrs Walker, after she and Hives had confirmed the identity of the body, prior to its removal and they had re-joined Cosmo and Izzie downstairs. Bobby had taken the old admiral home, but Cosmo assured them that they would return Izzie to the Crow's Nest, eventually.

"But we had a leaving party for her."

"And a whip round for a leaving present for her."

"And a fair-sized cheque for her pension fund for her."

"She went round the world. I had postcards of the Vatican

from Rome, the Cathedral of Santiago de Compostela."

"I had one from Lourdes, saying that she had prayed for my father."

"I had one from Las Vegas and another from Hawaii."

"I had one from Perth," said Mrs Walker.

"Western Australia?"

"No. Scotland."

"Well, she must have come back. We never did find her bunch of keys."

"Well," said Mrs Walker, "That will explain a lot of things-those phantom flushings, for a start."

Izzie, ever practical, asked: "Oh, you don't think she starved to death up there, poor thing?"

"I doubt it. There were unopened cases of Scotch in the room, as well as a crate of Crabbie's Ginger Wine. And boxes of Hobnobs."

"Well, at least she died happy." said Sir Cosmo.

The phone rang and Hives answered it.

When he came back into the room, he said that the BBC wanted an interview. They would have sent a helicopter to film the place from above but had cut back on such activities after an excess of zeal had cause a deal of expensive repercussions.

"How on earth can they interview me? I am not going into those dreadful studios they have in Plymouth."

"You could use my phone," suggested Izzie. "It has a movie camera. If they have the technology, we could do it right here."

Out on the moor, Auroch and Gaia had deposited Philip in the yurt that they hoped might be the start of a glamping business. Again, he was delighted.

"How did you know I shall probably be living in one of these soon? Getting me accustomed! Ulaan Bataar is renowned for its yurts. So thoughtful. How like the FO."

The other two were anxiously and more and more apprehensively awaiting the local news. The kidnapping of a lord, however little known, must have attracted some attention, as would the fire at the estate.

They had a variety of metal clothes hangers which, when suitably juxtaposed, could pick up just about anything from Freeview to Al Jazeera. It was just a matter of twiddling the hangers. Just in time, the image of the Mena Dhu woods with smoke drifting above them appeared between the lines, closely followed by a face they seemed to recognise.

"Lord de Coverlet," said the unseen interviewer, "can you tell us what happened?"

Confusion grew.

"'E's Lord de Coverlet!? Then ' oo's the one we got 'ere?"

"That Cyril sed 'e was the one."

"Is it on?" asked Cosmo," Oh, right. Good evening. Well, we have had quite a day. A most splendid village Fete then a brief *contre-temp*s as an ill-advise rat gnawed through some of the wiring and we had a bit of a fire, soon under control-again, our stout lads from the volunteer fire brigade did their stuff, of course, and now, it seems we are not exactly sure where my cousin, Philip, is at the moment but then there's nothing unusual about that. Goodnight." And he turned away from Izzie's camera to ask, "Do you think that was all right?" before the technicians in Television Centre could realise that he had finished and wasn't expecting any further questions.

Unfortunately, Cyril chose that time to arrive at the farmstead.

"But you're meant to be nationalists! Liberationists! You've got one of the oppressors!"

"Oppressors!? Phil couldn't oppress nothin; 'less it was a clutch pedal. Naow, 'E's great." said Tina.

"Knows a telescopic fork from a trailing link." said Brian. "Not every bugger can do that, nob or not."

"And what's all this crap about liberationists?" asked Tina.

"You're supposed to be Breder Kernow, after all!" This was the reason Cyril had chosen them, after all.

"Naow. That were the other people. Was 'ere before us. They moved." Auroch's bovine complacency was beginning to wear thin.

"Now you tell me! Where to?"

Cyril was losing it quickly.

"Brittany, I think. Said the French 'as revolutions regular- they got fed up with gettin' nowhere here. Gone over to join the Armorica Freedom Liberation front."

"Then who are you?"

"Small-holders from Erdington- gonna be bijou, luxury yurt glampers-" replied Gaia.

"Anyway, we got you a Coverlet- where's our monay?"

The only thing easily saleable was Cyril's Skoda Favourit; Auroch had a fairly new Autotrader magazine which quoted £550.

"That'll have to do. We'll keep it an' sell it" said Auroch."

"But what about me? How am I going to get back home for start?"

Auroch looked at Gaia.

"'f we put 'im in other yurt, I can drop 'im back when I fetch Phil 'ome in the morning."

"I knew it were too good to be true. I told yer, didn't I, I said it's too good to be true."

"Aye, luv, yaou did."

Back at Mena Dhu, they were about to settle back in the sitting room when Cosmo remembered.

"Are you something of a rat fan?" asked Cosmo.

"I'd nearly forgotten."

Quickly she removed the rigid little rodent from the bag, took one look and said:

"That's what I was afraid of. It's one of ours!"

"Ours?" asked Hives. "Do you collect them?"

"No, but the... the people I work with- or for- do. That was it!"

She slapped her head while the others looked on, lost.

"I knew I'd seen that face."

"Who?"

"Never mind. That's who it was. They breed these little chaps to crave the taste of electric wiring. A very convoluted dirty trick. That mean the fire was intentional. "

"Intentional?"

"And if it is them, there's going to be something else. Always a back-up. Belt and braces. Quick. We must search."

"What for?" asked Mrs Walker.

"I've no idea. Look for something that shouldn't be there."

"More rats?" asked Cosmo. "Or some other rodents? Coypus are very rare round here."

"No" said Izzie. "Have you got torches?"

"Indeed," replied Hives." Flaming or...?"

"Ordinary electric."

The butler concurred.

"Get them and then spread out. Start in the cellars. The wine cellar, I suggest. If that went up..."

It was a peculiar sight, the four of them hunting for they knew not what but the longer they took, the more desperate Izzy became. While not in detail, she obvious knew approximately who they were up against. Under wine racks, behind pillars, disturbing real, live civilian rats, shaking spiders out of sacks, torches in one hand and, in the case of Hives, a cricket bat in the other- the only immediate weapon his could find.

"You don't think they'd have sent in a squad of poisonous

spiders, do you?" asked Mrs Walker.

"Not unless they're a new string to their bow, as it were."

Nothing in the wine cellar. They went up to the ground floor and were passing the accounts room when Hives said:

"Best check- if we lost the Endowment Coffer we would be in a pickle."

It was Hives who found it.

"That wasn't there yesterday when we were doing the V.A.T."

It looked like a dog turd from a particularly large and healthy canine but also by one who packaged his stools very neatly.

"Don't worry, it won't be wired" said Izzie. "Simply set to a signal- possibly even a mobile phone. Fortunately, the signal's very weak in here. Let's just get it out of the place quickly."

"Izzie," said Sir Cosmo as they rushed out of the house, "Just in case... anything happens... Will... or rather... would you marry me?

"If anything happens, "she replied dourly, heading for the cliff... "There won't be anything left to marry."

"Well, would you have married me?" asked Cosmo, hoping his tenses were correct.

"Of course. Now- quick, Hives- the bat."

Izzie had taken command and Hives passed it to her.

"Now, on the previous display, I reckon I'm the best one to hit if you, Hives could lob it to me."

She exchanged the bomb for the bat.

"Nice and gentle- outside the off stump."

The butler bowled the bomb and Izzie belted it out into the night.

In the pub, a well-deserved aura of well-oiled satisfaction had spread. Again, there was little conversation.

"Well," said Charlie, his arm free from its sling and more than ready to pull pints. "That was something else."

Nobody spoke. They weren't all sure what he meant.

Suddenly a vast explosion lit up the bright sky, over by Mena Dhu.

"They didn't say nothing about fireworks," said Jago. "Selfish buggers, keepin' them to theyselves!"

Chapter Eighteen

But Izzy had a covert phone call to make before she could sit down with Mrs Walker and start discussing the intricacies of weddings. She wandered off into the woods and dialled a special number, one she remembered rather than had recorded anywhere.

When it was answered, she was no longer the perfect young naval officer.

"Yes, I am still here. No thanks to you. With one of your late pets. An ex-rat! And don't even start- I know SAS rats when I see them- two legged ones as well."

The man at the other end was quiet for a while and then asked: "Well?"

"I'm presuming this was... moon-lighting?"

"Unofficial overtime."

"Thought so. Otherwise you'd have had your boys with you. To keep you safe from harm."

"But it came from high up."

"I don't care if it came from fucking Edmund Hilary on the top of Mount Everest."

"They said something about him claiming to be the King of England."

"Did they? Then you're very lucky you fucked up cos the

punishment for regicide- killing kings, to you- is still hanging, drawing and quartering."

"Oh, but-"

"You have a decision to make. We either hear- very soon- of the sad demise of an unsung national hero who was unbeknownst to anyone, suffering from such a bad dose of PTSD that he topped himself, namely you."

"Or?"

"The equally sad and rapid death of whoever put you up to this. Short of Prince Charles. And I should imagine that someone who needs a flunky to put toothpaste on his toothbrush for him isn't likely to know anything about the likes of us."

"How?"

"However you like. As spectacular or as trivial as you like. Just soon, and sure you get everyone who knows. Otherwise I'll be after you and spank your botty."

Really, it was only because Mark Tregaskis had originally come from Cornwall that the event was reported locally at all.

More important was the headline "Reclusive Lord to Wed," with the brief statement:

"The engagement is announced of Cosmo, only son of Lord Cosmo de Coverlet of Mena Dhu, Cornwall to Lt. Commander Isolde Hawkins, grand-daughter of Vice-Admiral Robert Hawkins of Crow's Nest, Porthwallow, Cornwall. Date to be announced."

This was followed by a gushing but flimsy article by Tilly Trellisk, the paper's social editor who had struggled to find a hundred words to write, so little was known about either of the lovebirds.

It had been a lot easier for the editor to fill his column under the headline; Mysterious Death of Cornish Civil Servant, explaining that Police are still investigating the sudden deaths of two senior Civil Servants, one Mark Tregaskis, a Camborne boy who had made good in London, and a colleague, Catriona Douglas, who had no obvious connection with the Duchy. The fact that they both suffered similar heart-attacks on the same day cannot be overlooked. There is no suggestion of impropriety in their relationship, but the Head of Flying Squad has refused to rule out any Bulgarian connection. That was all he was allowed to write. The D notice had come as something of a surprise. Even at 'Private Eye' they had been rather miffed.

Next morning Philip strode back up the drive to Mena Dhu, still in his cricket whites and blazer but with a smile on his face.

He was an MGB Roadster this morning, with the top down.

Cosmo and, to Philip's mild surprise, Izzy were still at breakfast. She was wearing something of Mrs Walker's and looked like a child in her granny's dressing gown. As usual, the chafing dishes were loaded and he started to serve himself.

"Philip!" cried Cosmo. "Where have you been?"

"F.O. special training. At least, I think that's what it must have been. Drove a Morris 7 van, which I suppose is the nearest thing we have here to what they'll have out there, their Mongolian jalopies. Spent the night in a yurt. Something I suppose I shall have to get used to. And the bloody awful food. They actually had a sort of muesli which seemed to consist mainly of grit. Leastways, the chickens were very interested in it."

"But you're all right?"

"Fine. Morning, Miss Hawkins. Miss your bus?"

"Good morning, Mr de Coverlet. Something like that, yes."

"There is a most remarkable smell in the air this morning, Cosmo. Smells like high explosive. Can that fire really have left that sort of pong? By the way, how's Uncle?"

"As far as we can tell, fine. His outing seems to have done him good."

"So, all's well that ends well, I suppose. Haven't really seen you since the cricket. Match tied. By Jove, cracking good game. Do you think they play it in Mongolia?"

"Not sure."

"The Afghans have a jolly good team." This from Izzy. "I watched a few games when I was out there."

"Afghanistan's not on the sea, is it?" Philip could be quick when need be.

"Ah... no. No. I was there as a sort of... adviser."

"But they don't have a navy, at least, as far as I know," said Philip, now into his toast and marmalade. Cook had a secret recipe for her marmalade which, she has sworn, will go with her to the grave.

"Afghanistan. They haven't sent me there yet," added Philip. Izzy felt he was getting too close so she turned to Hives. "I say, is there any chance of some more coffee?"

Philip was thus distracted and eventually packed off to London with a word of advice from Izzy.

"Really, I think the less said about your... adventures the better. If I'm not mistaken, you're right and it was part of a hush-hush exercise, accustoming you to what you might experience out there."

"Thought so. I say, is it true you're going to marry the Cuz?"

"How did you hear that?" she asked.

"Ah," said Philip. "Fieldcraft, my dear. Fieldcraft. Do let me know when, and I'll try to wangle some leave. Um..." And here he went through the whole rigmarole of being embarrassed. If he had been wearing a tie, he would have wiggled the end like Oliver Hardy. "I don't suppose there are any more at home like you, are there? I mean, crikey, I think Cosmo's bloody lucky."

Izzy kissed him on the cheek.

"I'll check the cupboard."

Chapter Nineteen

It looks as though Auroch and Gaia are going to make a go of their bijou 'glampsite', greatly aided by a very generous mysterious donation. Philip had no idea of their address, or whether they possessed a bank account and had only a very vague idea of where he had been, but the hand-painted posters advertising 'logins' in yurts had helped Hives to find his way when delivering the suitcase which he left outside the gate.

Discussions about the forthcoming wedding in the pub, *The Copper Kettle*, *The Crow's Nest* and not surprisingly, Mena Dhu, eclipsed those that had been generated by other, earlier, higher profile weddings up country. They completely obliterated any concern or even interest in Britain's future involvement in Europe. Here they were involved; there, there was nothing they could do about it.

"Given who he is and that," said Jago, "he's every right to ask for Westminster Abbey. I mean, if these... 'Johnny-come-latelies' can all get wed there-"

"Charles and Diana were St Paul's." offered Jeremy.

"Some were done at St George's Chapel at Windsor," said Tegan, who knew about such things.

"Yeah, but I bet that was just to save Her Majesty and Philip from getting out of bed too early. I mean, they are getting on-" The Vicar always tried to see both sides of the argument.

"Are you gonna do them?" asked H.

"Marry them? Oh, I do hope so, but the announcement was only last week. I suppose I could drop them a note, saying the diary's pretty empty between now and Christmas if they want to have St Wallow's."

"Reckon it's be that quick?"

"Well, they do say Cosmo's looking for an heir and I just can't see that Izzy comin' down the aisle with a bun in the oven. It may be all right for some people we know but not aristocracy."

"Bugger aristocracy; they'm royal!"

"Where" was also a subject under discussion at the Big House, prompted and attended by Trevor.

Izzy seemed to be on almost permanent leave from the Navy and so, quite rightly, was in on all the plans.

"Somebody from the Bishop's palace in Truro rang," said Cosmo. "Offering the Cathedral but I'm afraid I made an executive decision and declined the offer. I trust that is all right, my dear?" Such terms of endearment were new to Cosmo's lips and still sounded rather stilted.

"AOK with me."

"So the question is, St Wallow's or do we just open up the Chapel here?"

"It rather depends," said Hives, "on how many guests you were intending to invite, Sir."

"Well, we can hardly turn away the village, can we and they would certainly not all fit into the Oratory. And some of them might feel a little uncomfortable knowing that they are standing, or sitting on the bones of so many of my ancestors. In fact, I don't think there's any one of them missing down there since they built the place in the sixteenth century."

"I wonder if they would all get into St Wallow's."

"Trevor?" asked Sir Cosmo.

"Well, the only time we ever get anything near a full house is Midnight Mass at Christmas and a lot of them are second-home owners, down for the festivities. Normally we're pushed to make double figures. Not counting the Harvest festival. Of course, but much of that was the Michael influence."

"Oh, but we must have Michael," said Izzy. Even though a ruthless member of one of the world's finest armed forces, she was still female and Michael had had an effect on her, same as on almost all other women.

"I'm not sure we want pop songs at a wedding," tried Cosmos, but as with almost everything else, Izzy knew her subject.

"Don't forget he was a Cathedral chorister. He's bound to know something apart from his greatest hits. Although after..." And here she dried up for fear of appearing overzealous. After all, it was her wedding they were discussing.

"Do you know 'Amazing Grace'? I know it's rather old hat,

but I find it's an excellent go-to when nothing else obvious appears."

"Details," said Cosmo and the subject was dropped.

"Excuse me Miss, "said Mrs Walker," but are you intending to wear white?"

"Absolutely," said Izzy, brazen-faced, while Cosmo blushed into the handkerchief.

"In that case, would you like the dress made... 'in-house'? Cook and I have already-"

"Oh but that is so kind of you, Mrs W. but when I say 'white' I mean my tropical No. 1 dress uniform. Trousers and all. Very smart. Smartest thing I've got. Somehow I don't feel quite... unassailable in a frock."

"How about," began Hives, who had not been involved in the subject of the frock, "if we have a service at the church and possibly a bit of a do at the pub, overseen by Charley while a smaller, select few come up here for a blessing, or something, in the Oratory. Then the ancestors wouldn't feel out of it and Cook would not have to cater for the entire village."

"Now that," said Cosmo, "I like."

They did not send invitations except to the few who had been essential and that was for the Blessing at the Big House, followed by the wedding breakfast that night, but made it known that everyone would be welcome at St Wallow. The fact that it was a mile or two outside the village again raised a clamour in *The Copper Kettle* when it was said that it was too far even for those with mobility scooters, but when Mr Hives let it be known that the old bus was being licensed again, especially for the occasion and that Cousin Philip would be driving- his ban having somehow been rescinded- then they had to find other subjects to grumble about.

Mr and Mrs Charlie at *The Coverlet Arms* had discovered a five figure sum had been paid into their account and several trays full of Cook's finest pasties were to be delivered that day, which meant that Mrs Charlie and her staff could concentrate on a right royal spread. It was a free bar which some abused but for the most part, they drank to the health of the not-so-young couple with restraint.

And to avoid any unpleasantness, it just so happened that, that weekend, Inspector Foot was sent to the Brecon Beacons on a training course essential for any hope of promotion. While Cyril Oliphant received a surprise voucher for an 'all expenses paid' two-day break in Rhyll, something that he intended on exploiting to the full.

The Chapel at Mena Dhu seldom saw services of any sort, with the rare exception of funerals after which the principal figures tended to be deposited below. It made a pleasant exception, then, that, on this occasion, they all- with the exception of the Admiral who stuck to his scooter, even when leading Izzy down the aisle- walked out of the Oratory.

And the Admiral, accompanied by the Cook, followed

Cosmo and Izzy and behind them, Bobby and Tegan, Michael and Sandy, H. and his wife Bev, who couldn't believe her luck, Hives and Mrs Walker, and lastly Trevor and Jeremy across the lawn and into the Big House through the main front door, opened for once in respect for this very special occasion. All two by two, rather like the animals into the Ark.

All except for Jago who stood alone on Tristan's Leap and looked away to the South East, toward the onion fields of Roscoff and the distant lights of the *Folies Bergeres*, remembering.